Blotto, Twinks and the
Dead Dowager Duchess

BLOTTO, TWINKS AND THE DEAD DOWAGER DUCHESS

Simon Brett

FELONY & MAYHEM PRESS • NEW YORK

All the characters and events portrayed in this work are fictitious.

BLOTTO, TWINKS AND THE DEAD DOWAGER DUCHESS

A Felony & Mayhem mystery

PRINTING HISTORY
First U.K. edition (Constable): 2010
Felony & Mayhem edition: 2012

Copyright © 2010 by Simon Brett

ISBN: 978-1-934609-92-7

Manufactured in the United States of America

Printed on 100% recycled paper

Library of Congress Cataloging-in-Publication Data

Brett, Simon.
Blotto, Twinks and the dead dowager duchess / Simon Brett. -- 1st Felony
& Mayhem ed.
    p. cm.
ISBN 978-1-934609-92-7
1. Brothers and sisters--Fiction. 2. Murder--Investigation--Fiction. I. Title.
PR6052.R4296B564 2012
823'.914--dc23
                        2011044656

To Louise, who enjoys a good laugh.

The icon above says you're holding a book in the Felony & Mayhem "British" category. These books are set in or around the UK, and feature the highly literate, often witty prose that fans of British mystery demand. If you enjoy this book, you may well like other "British" titles from Felony & Mayhem Press.

———◆———

For information about British titles or to learn more about Felony & Mayhem Press, please visit us online at:

www.FelonyAndMayhem.com

Or write to us at:

Felony and Mayhem Press
156 Waverly Place
New York, NY 10014

Other "British" titles from

FELONY&MAYHEM

MICHAEL DAVID ANTHONY
The Becket Factor
Midnight Come
Dark Provenance

ROBERT BARNARD
Corpse in a Gilded Cage
Death and the Chaste Apprentice
Death on the High C's
The Skeleton in the Grass
Out of the Blackout

SIMON BRETT
Blotto, Twinks and the Ex-King's
Daughter

DUNCAN CAMPBELL
If It Bleeds

KATE CHARLES
A Drink of Deadly Wine

PETER DICKINSON
King and Joker
The Old English Peep Show
Skin Deep
Sleep and His Brother

CAROLINE GRAHAM
The Killings at Badger's Drift
Death of a Hollow Man
Death in Disguise
Written in Blood
Murder at Madingley Grange

REGINALD HILL
A Clubbable Woman
An Advancement of Learning
Ruling Passion
An April Shroud
A Killing Kindness
Deadheads
Exit Lines
Child's Play
Under World

ELIZABETH IRONSIDE
The Accomplice
The Art of Deception
Death in the Garden
A Very Private Enterprise

BARRY MAITLAND
The Marx Sisters
The Chalon Heads

SHEILA RADLEY
Death in the Morning
The Chief Inspector's Daughter
A Talent for Destruction
Fate Worse than Death

L.C. TYLER
The Herring Seller's Apprentice
Ten Little Herrings
The Herring in the Library

LOUISE WELSH
Naming the Bones

Blotto, Twinks and the
Dead Dowager Duchess

Chapter One

To Snitterings

If there was one thing Blotto (properly known as the Honourable Devereux Lyminster) didn't like about weekend house parties, it was the inevitable gathering-together of a large number of people with dark secrets in their past, along with the tiresome near-certainty that one of them would get murdered. Not to mention the unavoidable presence of a know-it-all polymathic amateur sleuth who would happen to be staying for the weekend. And the obligatory moment when the aforementioned know-it-all polymathic amateur sleuth would dragoon everyone into the library to tell them whodunit.

So Blotto didn't like going away to weekend house parties. In fact, he didn't really like going away anywhere. Everything he loved and needed—like cricket and hunting—was readily available at his ancestral family home, Tawcester Towers.

But *noblesse oblige* and all that rombooley. When his mother, the Dowager Duchess of Tawcester, announced that she,

Blotto and his sister Twinks (properly known as Lady Honoria Lyminster) were going to spend a weekend at Snitterings, the ancestral family home of that premier Catholic family the Melmonts, he knew where his duty lay. He also knew, from long experience, the hopelessness of any attempts to go against his mother's wishes. The Dowager Duchess had certain physical characteristics in common with a Mark IV tank, and was equally difficult to deflect from her chosen course.

She also had another purpose that was ominous to Blotto. His mother prided herself on her match-making skills and the Melmont family boasted a daughter called Laetitia who was very definitely in the marriage market. In fact, she'd been in the marriage market since anyone could remember. She had been on the shelf so long that she was suffering from an advanced case of mildew.

An attempt had been made to hitch Laetitia Melmont up to Blotto straight after she'd 'come out', and he remembered thinking at the time that, so far as he was concerned, he just wished she'd go back in again. He'd yet to find in any woman those fine qualities of loyalty and companionship that you found in a good horse.

On that occasion the ghastly fate of matrimony had been avoided, but Blotto didn't dare let his guard drop. To his mother an idea was like a bone to a terrier; however many times it got buried, it could still be dug up and chewed over again.

Blotto had once put to her what he thought was the rather cunning argument that he shouldn't marry Laetitia because she was Catholic. 'Oh, that doesn't matter the way it used to,' the Dowager Duchess had replied airily. 'The rules of society have relaxed considerably. These days people of our sort are even marrying Americans.' Blotto should have known that there was never any way of getting round his mother.

So when she announced that they were going to Snitterings for a long weekend—Thursday afternoon to Sunday, for heaven's sake—to Snitterings they went. The Dowager Duchess had been with Pansy Melmont at one of those convent schools where girls of the right sort are taught to talk very loudly, wear tweed and sneer at their inferiors. Pansy had been skilfully manoeuvred by her parents into marriage to the Duke of Melmont. That unfortunate peer having succumbed to an excess of port and chambermaids, she had found herself in later life, like Blotto and Twinks's mother, with the title of Dowager Duchess. And Blotto's mother was a great believer in the principle that Dowager Duchesses should stick together.

Blotto had wanted to drive over to Snitterings alone in the Lagonda, but his mother slapped a veto on that little plan. She suspected (quite rightly) that, given his own transport, Blotto would spend as much time away from Snitterings on various errands as he possibly could. She therefore mandated that she, Blotto and Twinks would all travel together in one of the Tawcester Towers Rolls-Royces, with Corky Froggett acting as chauffeur.

Corky Froggett was a military man. Prepared from birth to give his all for King and Country, he was unable to disguise his disappointment when in 1918 King and Country had put an end to the war he was enjoying so much. A practical man, though, he did not brood on this setback, immediately transferring his undying loyalty from King and Country to his employers, the Lyminster family at Tawcester Towers. As he never ceased to tell them, he would readily lay down his life for any one of them. His only complaint about his life was that so few opportunities for laying it down occurred in the normal course of his chauffeuring duties.

Corky Froggett had the voice of a lovable cockney, but the killing instinct of a piranha that had just had a row with its wife. His black uniform covered a body so muscular that bumping into it could cause serious damage to the bumper-into. And though he was loyal to every member of the family at Tawcester Towers, Blotto was the one to whom Corky Froggett saw himself as unofficial bodyguard.

There was a logic to this. The Dowager Duchess cut such a daunting figure that no one had ever dared to threaten her. A look from her piercing blue eyes could freeze a tiger in midleap—and had once done so during a day's hunting with the Maharajah of Pranjipur.

Her elder son, Rupert Lyminster Duke of Tawcester, universally known as 'Loofah', did not need much protection either. His was not a personality full of get-up-and-go. He was more full of I-think-I'll-stay-here-thank-you-very-much. Though he was entitled to attend the House of Lords and shape the future of his nation, he very rarely did. The only date on which he was guaranteed to be there was the Wednesday before Christmas when there was always a rather good Christmas lunch. In fact, the only—and indeed the greatest—challenge of Loofah's life was to impregnate his angularly unappealing wife, known as 'Sloggo', with something that didn't turn out to be another girl, and thus ensure the continuation of the Tawcester dynasty.

So that left his two younger siblings, and though Blotto and his sister both got involved in hazardous scrapes, Twinks was far too intelligent to put herself in unnecessary danger. Her brother, on the other hand, approached unnecessary danger with the lip-smacking relish most people reserve for a cream tea. It was for this reason that having Corky Froggett to keep a protective eye on Blotto was entirely essential.

The drive from Tawcester Towers to Snitterings on the Thursday afternoon was not filled with the sparkle of conversation. The Dowager Duchess slept, her snores shuddering through the leather upholstery of the Rolls-Royce like a stampede of distant wildebeest. Twinks, who was a bit of a brainbox, was reading Thucydides' *History of the Peloponnesian War* in the original Greek, one of the many objects she kept in her reticule, while Blotto looked disconsolately out of the car window. He wasn't much of a one for books. At least there was one called *The Hand of Fu Manchu* which he was quite enjoying, but he'd been reading it for two years and hadn't got halfway yet.

All he really wanted to do at that moment was be back at Tawcester Towers, preferably out in the field astride his splendid hunter, Mephistopheles. There was nothing at Snitterings that he looked forward to seeing, least of all Laetitia. He had detected a new purposeful beadiness in the Dowager Duchess of Tawcester's eye, and feared it was not unconnected to match-making.

Broken biscuits, what a gluepot, thought Blotto miserably. This weekend house party's going to be about as much fun as a convention of undertakers. His impossibly handsome brow under its fine crest of blond hair wrinkled with distaste. His fine blue eyes lost their customary sparkle. Blotto's brain wasn't often troubled by thoughts, and most of those which did flit through the vacancy of his cranium were of an extremely cheering kind. But the one big thought that filled every cranny of his mind at that moment—the thought of going to Snitterings—really vinegared him off.

After Corky Froggett had brought the Rolls-Royce to a perfect stop on the arc of gravel in front of the great house, he opened the doors to let out his passengers. The two Dowager Duchesses approached each other like a pair of mastodons with pearl necklaces and territorial ambitions. Under the Dowager Duchess of Melmont's arm was clutched her adored Pekinese Clutterbuck. His poppy eyes and squashed-in face perfectly matched in miniature the features of his mistress.

Since they had met at school, the friendship of the two aristocrats had always been based on intense rivalry. The Dowager Duchess of Tawcester had captured her Duke first, during the season in which she 'came out', and from that moment on Pansy had been determined to bag one of her own. It took a couple of years before she got her claws into the Duke of Melmont and since then, in the view of the Dowager Duchess of Tawcester, her rival had been just playing catch-up.

The pair greeted each other at the entrance to Snitterings with smiles that could have frosted hot toddies. Each kissed the air at some distance from the other's heavily powdered face. 'How brave of you to wear mauve,' the Dowager Duchess of Tawcester boomed at her friend. 'It certainly brings out your complexion.'

'And how clever of your dressmaker,' the Dowager Duchess of Melmont honked back, 'to come up with a gown which makes it look as though you actually have a waist.'

These pleasantries exchanged, the two combatants advanced into the splendid interior of the house. Twinks looked back at her brother, dawdling with all the reluctance of a new bug at the beginning of term. She held out the hand that wasn't holding her Thucydides. 'Come on, Blotto me old gumdrop. Just think, in three days' time, you'll be back lighting the fireworks of fun at Tawcester Towers. You'll be able to forget this weekend ever happened.'

Blotto grinned ruefully at his sister. She was a Grade A Foundation Stone, old Twinks, always ready to give her big brother a jockey-up. A breathsapper of a beauty too, he thought, as the afternoon sun gleamed off the ash-blonde of her hair, and her perfect azure eyes beamed encouragement towards him.

'Nice of you to try and bolster my sagging spirits, Twinks me old bloater,' he said, 'but I've a nasty feeling that this time Mater and the Melmont hippo mean business.'

'Laetitia?'

He nodded the nod of a man whose life sentence has just been commuted to hanging.

'Oh, come on, you can get out of it, Blotto. You've managed before. Remember when Mater and the Melmont monster locked you and Laetitia into a Brighton hotel room and invited press photographers along? You got out of that by changing clothes with a member of the staff. And the Sunday smut-rags got their juicy story of a Duke's daughter having a fling with a boot-boy. You've beaten the Dowager Duchesses before, Blotto me old whiffler, and you can do it again.'

'I don't know. Mater has in her eyes the look of an anaconda that's identified the cow it's going to swallow and live off for the next month. And in this case, I'm the cow.'

'Oh, look, Blotters, you don't even like Laetitia. You can't let her be stuck on you like an unwanted corn plaster. Laetitia's a—'

But even as Twinks spoke, the subject of their conversation came skittering down the main steps of Snitterings, smiling winsomely and giving Blotto yet another opportunity to assess the threat she posed to his happiness.

The Dowager Duchess of Melmont's daughter's heart may have been in the right place, but providence had been a little random in the disposition of her other body parts. She in fact looked like the Netherlands, completely lacking in contours (so much so that at school—and indeed for a long time thereafter—she had had the nickname of 'the Snitterings Ironing-Board'). Her face bore the pallor of wallpaper that had had the sun on it too long. And her teeth were of a size to make piano tuners come over all wistful. Add to this a voice which could have sand-blasted the south elevation of Westminster Cathedral and you begin to have an accurate estimation of her charms.

But it wasn't Laetitia's looks that put Blotto off the idea of marrying her. He had, after all, watched his brother Loofah bite the rather long bullet that was his wife Sloggo. Blotto knew that, for people like him, the right bloodline in a spouse was infinitely more important than such evanescent details as physical charms. It was nothing personal. Laetitia didn't put him off. It was the very idea of matrimony always that made him feel like he'd swallowed the whole lemon.

Once on the gravel drive, Laetitia gambolled towards them like a particularly girlish lamb. Even Blotto, the most chivalrous of men, was unable to suppress the thought that girlish gambolling was not the ideal style of movement for a woman of her proportions.

From long experience, he tensed his leg muscles in anticipation of the vocal typhoon ahead. Twinks, unprepared and slighter in physique, bent daintily backwards like a sapling as Laetitia began to speak.

'Blotto! Twinks! Darlings!' she bellowed at them. 'It's simply scrumplicious to have you here at Snitterings!' She enveloped Twinks in the kind of embrace sea anemones reserve for particularly slow shrimps.

She then turned to Blotto. Before she could repeat the sea anemone manoeuvre he stretched out his hand. Disappointed, Laetitia took it. Hers in his felt like uncooked veal.

'Oh, Blotto!' She fluttered eyelashes like woodshavings at him, before blaring out, 'Isn't it wonderful? A whole long weekend! Now we'll really have a chance to get to know each other!'

He caught the look of pitying amusement in his sister's azure eyes as feebly he enthused, 'Pure strawberry jam with dollops of cream, Laetitia.'

Blotto wasn't very good at having new thoughts. So he had the same one again: Broken biscuits, what a gluepot.

Chapter Two

Romance in the Air

Dinner that Thursday evening at Snitterings made Napoleon's retreat from Moscow look like the height of jollity. While the two Dowager Duchesses sniped endlessly at each other, Blotto had to keep trying to avoid the gaze of the besotted Laetitia. He thought she was probably trying to make cow's eyes at him, but her physical limitations prevented her from coming up with anything better than frog's eyes.

Twinks wasn't faring much better at her side of the table. The current Duke of Melmont was, like his sister, as yet unmarried, and he had invited down some of his former Harrovian friends 'to liven things up'. For Blotto, an Eton man, their presence was about as welcome as a slug in the shower. What's more, he quickly established that none of the stenchers had played or even liked cricket. In fact, like the Duke their host, none of them had ever displayed any talent for anything other than spending their large inherited fortunes.

They were all large young men with protruding elbows and knees who, in common with most of their class, had never progressed beyond adolescence. Braying unintelligible anecdotes about their school days, all of which prompted fusillades of raucous laughter, they behaved as British public school boys normally do in the presence of a beautiful woman. They blushed, sniggered, and muttered hilarity-inducing innuendoes behind their hands. Twinks, with one of the young blades either side of her, found the whole business very tiresome.

To cast an even deeper shadow over the evening there was present, as Blotto had gloomily anticipated, a know-it-all polymathic amateur sleuth who just happened to be staying for the weekend. Troubadour Bligh was a small man in tight-cut dapper evening dress and spats (which even Blotto, who never took much interest in protocol, knew were inappropriate for dinner wear). The sleuth affected long silver hair and a golden monocle. His fingers bore far more rings than a gentleman would wear and—to add to his social solecisms—there was an aura of lavender water around him. Blotto was the most reasonable of men is most respects, but when it came to scent...well, he did feel quite strongly that chaps should smell of chap and nothing else.

Troubadour Bligh, though without breeding of any kind—and dining amongst his betters—still had no inhibitions about dominating the conversation at dinner. All he could talk about was his prowess as an investigator. His voice too grated; it was high-pitched and quick, sounding more like a woman's than a man's. Blotto had heard dark rumours at school that there were some chaps who were more like women than men in other details than their voices. Before, he had always dismissed the notion as completely outside the rule book, but as the sleuth prattled girlishly about another of his investigations, Troubadour Bligh made him wonder.

'Of course the Belgian police were at their wits' end—not that they had to go very far to reach them—and they begged—no, they implored—me to cast my beady little eye over the scene of the crime. Well, I'd intended my time at Ostend to be complete relaxation—after all I'd just solved the Case of the Patagonian Three-Legged Jaguar—but they were so insistent—almost pathetic in their entreaties—that I said I would. The first thing I noticed—which of course nobody else had picked up—was that the top had never been *on* the bottle of ink. In fact it belonged to a different bottle of ink completely, which had been substituted for the one on the Countess's escritoire. It took only a sniff of the ink for me to recognize the distinctive aroma of a poison extracted from the sap of the Upholas tree by the Aspoko tribesmen deep in the heart of the Amazonian jungle. As I'm sure you know, Upholas resin is fatal not only when ingested, but also if it gets into the bloodstream through an open wound, however small. A scratch by a bramble, even a pinprick could prove fatal if it was touched by the poison. Suddenly it was clear to me why the short-sighted Countess's nail brush had been replaced by a cheese grater, causing those minuscule abrasions on the fingers of her left—left, I say, her *writing* hand. The Belgian police could not believe how quickly I was able to point a finger at the perpetrator of this...'

And so he droned on. Blotto shuddered inwardly. Being stuck at Snitterings really was the flea's armpit. Even without the threat of a simpering Laetitia hovering on the edge of his peripheral vision. The normally heart-warming prospect of hunting on the Saturday didn't cheer him up that much. The hunting wouldn't be as good as it was at Tawcester Towers— nowhere was it as good as it was at Tawcester Towers. And no animal the Snitterings stables might come up with could match the majesty of Mephistopheles.

Everything about the weekend was so predictable. Particularly the presence of the repellent Troubadour Bligh. The first few times he'd gone to a weekend house party at a stately home where there was a know-it-all polymathic amateur sleuth present, Blotto had been quite excited when the murder finally happened. Now, as an entertainment, it was as commonplace as Musical Chairs at a tot's birthday party. Blotto could hardly summon up the energy to cast an eye round the dinner guests, wondering which one of them would be bumped off. Mind you, when his scrutiny landed on the Duke's school chums, he could think of a few suitable candidates.

His look around the table had the unfortunate, but entirely predictable, effect of making him catch Laetitia's eye. She clearly thought this was deliberate, and simpered winsomely. Now, in Blotto's view, there were very few women in the world who could get away with winsomeness, and Laetitia Melmont belonged firmly to that vast majority who couldn't. His only comfort was that it would soon be time for the ladies to withdraw. Thank God for that tradition. At least it dictated that men and women should have some respite from each other's company.

But the cheer he took from that was short-lived. He couldn't even look forward to the welcome release of a few quiet brandies in the billiard room after the ladies retired. In all probability the loathsome Troubadour Bligh would adjourn there too. And, even if he didn't, the Duke's cronies would no doubt make the atmosphere insufferable with their reminiscences of torturing new bugs, and their off-colour jokes about that Great Unknown Territory—women. Then it would only be a matter of time before they started throwing billiard balls at the Snitterings fine collection of Old Masters.

Blotto felt extremely vinegared off.

The Friday lived up to the ghastliness of the Thursday evening. There was nothing for Blotto to do. November was the wrong time of year for cricket, and from what the other guests were saying, he gathered there wouldn't have been a match even in the summer. The Duke's pusillanimous dislike of the game at Harrow had stayed with him for life, and his cronies were equally antipathetic. This disturbed Blotto. He could never really trust a man who didn't like cricket.

There was tennis, however. Really a summer game, but the Snitterings groundsmen had kept the grass of the courts in fine trim. Though of course he and Twinks played to international standard, Blotto had always dismissed tennis as a 'woman's game'. Still, better than nothing. A vigorous half-dozen sets might help to dissipate the unaccustomed gloom that was building within him.

But, unfortunately, Laetitia was present when the idea of tennis was proposed. 'Oh, how scrumplicious!' she boomed. 'We can take on all comers in the Mixed Doubles, can't we, Blotto?'

'Well, er, um...' He tried desperately to invent an excuse, but he couldn't without lying. And Blotto didn't like lying. This was partly due to his being an English gentleman, but also because he had a fatal tendency to forget what lie he'd actually told and end up in some ghastly gluepot as a result.

'That'd be really hoopee-doopee!' Laetitia went on. 'I'm sure we'll make a teriffulous pairing, Blotto.' Her pale lashes twitched like moths caught in a spider's web. 'In tennis, *as in everything else.*' On these last words she dropped her voice so low it could only be heard one county away.

Blotto couldn't come up with anything other than another 'Well, er, um...'

Now, he knew that not everyone could be as naturally gifted at sports as he and Twinks, but he'd never encountered anyone with as little instinct for tennis as Laetitia Melmont. Her favoured serve was a double fault, and it never seemed to occur to her to move towards where the ball was going to land. Even when the pill came straight at her, nine times out of ten she missed it. As a result, Blotto had to cover the whole court like a demented bluebottle to avoid their being thrashed. Fortunately he was a good enough player to compensate for his partner's deficiencies and they managed to emerge as winners.

What was embarrassing about the situation, though, was that Laetitia regarded every point he salvaged as an act of chivalry. He was her White Knight, doing everything for her. This put Blotto into something of a fire and frying pan dilemma. His natural sporting instinct made him rush for every ball like a cheetah on spikes, even though he knew that every successful retrieval was being interpreted by his partner as further proof of his love for her. He was as torn as a vegetarian cannibal.

Meanwhile on the adjacent court, Twinks, in a tennis dress as diaphanous as thistledown, proceeded to give lessons in singles to the Duke's old Harrovian chums. Each of them lumbered on to the court, confident of trouncing the slight figure at the other end. And each of them reckoned that a victory on the tennis court would give them some sort of seigneurial claims on their defeated opponent. Though none of the chaps had actually spent much time with girls, they all knew that there was nothing an attractive filly liked better than a sporting hero. Once they'd shown Twinks their prowess on the tennis court, she'd melt into their arms like a chocolate mousse in a hot marquee.

As each of them in turn dragged their aching bodies off the court, of course something else had happened. It wasn't only in their scores that love had featured so prominently, it was also in their hearts. They had all fallen madly in love with Twinks. It was inevitable. Her exertions had brought a new rosiness to her perfect cheeks, and her victories a new sparkle to her azure eyes. The Duke's Harrovian chums could no more have resisted falling in love with her than ageing jockeys could resist bribes.

And every one of them had as much chance of engaging Twinks's affections as a greengrocer does of joining a gentlemen's club.

The Friday evening's dinner was even more excruciating than the Thursday's. Prompted no doubt by Laetitia, the Dowager Duchess of Melmont had arranged the *placement* so that her daughter was actually sitting next to Blotto. Now, to add to the attempted cow's eyes directed at him throughout the meal, if he ever let his hand rest for more than a second on the crisp linen of the cloth he had to deal with a veal-like hand placed on top of it. And beneath the table one of Laetitia's substantial legs kept trying to coil itself around his dress trousering. The horror of the situation struck Blotto dumb.

Since the Duke's Old Harrovian chums spent the entire dinner gazing in soupy silence at his sister, conversation round the table flowed like congealed gravy. The Duke seemed to have caught his friends' affliction. Mouth agape over his non-existent chin, his fish-eyes too were fixed on the object of their fantasies. Twinks herself was far too used to this happening to be fazed by it, but if no one was going to make conversation to her, she didn't feel in the mood to make any back.

As a result, the only voices that could be heard were those of the two Dowager Duchesses exchanging decorous insults.

'How unfortunate, Evadne,' the Dowager Duchess of Melmont would say, 'that the Lyminster Rubies can't be seen at their best, being so close in colour to your complexion.'

'I'd rather have that, Pansy,' the Dowager Duchess of Tawcester would respond, 'than wear a pearl tiara that's exactly the same colour as my hair.'

Blotto caught another burst of frog-eye from Laetitia. He winced inwardly and tried to stop the wince from showing outwardly. As he felt the toes of a large foot tickle his leg above his sock suspenders, he began to think of the next day's hunting in a more favourable light. The sport might not be up to what was available at Tawcester Towers, but at least he'd heard Laetitia say firmly that she didn't like hunting and wouldn't be participating. He would get some time away from her cloying presence. At least that was something to look forward to.

But even as he had this comforting thought, he felt the blast of her voice in his ear. 'You know I said I always hated hunting...'

'Yes.'

'Well, I always have, but I think that's simply because I've never done it in the right company.'

'Oh?'

'I'm sure if I went hunting with *you*, Blotto, I'd really enjoy it.'

'Oh, I don't think you—'

'No, my mind's made up. I am going hunting with you tomorrow.'

The outward wince which he had been restraining all evening shuddered across Blotto's face.

He hadn't slept well either night at Snitterings. The room he'd been allocated was not one of the best. The front-facing bedrooms of the house commanded a splendid view over miles of unspoilt Melmontshire countryside. Blotto had got one at the back. The only view it commanded was of the stables, the garages, the kitchen garden and the outdoor privies (still used by the estate workers, who were not allowed to bring their muddy, clumping hobnails inside the house proper).

The room was tall, gaunt and chilly. Though the autumn days were warm, by night cold draughts infiltrated their way into Snitterings through ill-fitting window frames, slid along the cracks under doors and joined together into malevolent winds which moaned through the corridors and galleries of the place. The bedding in Blotto's bedroom smelt musty with damp.

Nor throughout the night was there ever a moment's silence. Snitterings was an old house and its component parts creaked like the limbs of an ancient man. Any running of a tap or flushing of a lavatory was the cue for a fifteen-minute concerto of clanging, drumming and gurgling. From the bedrooms of both Dowager Duchesses, rivals even in their snoring, the sound as of approaching earthquakes rumbled through the house. Sometimes Blotto's sleep would be disturbed by the shriek of a chambermaid, whose bedroom had been invaded by one of the Duke's Old Harrovian cronies (fortunately too drunk to offer any threat to the girl). And of course after five in the morning, when the staff rose, the clattering, clanking and banging from downstairs made further repose impossible.

It didn't seem like it, but Blotto must have slept a little, because at some point he woke up. And he woke up with a stuffed head and a streaming nose. Two nights in the damp sheets of Snitterings had given him a cold.

Now normally he wouldn't even have considered such a trifle. Blotto did not indulge in fripperies like pain. After all, hadn't he once steered the Eton First Eleven to victory with an unbeaten hundred and seventeen, only to discover later that he'd done it with a broken ankle? Hadn't he won the Two Hundred Yards Dash with four cracked ribs? A trifle like a cold was never going to keep Blotto from a day's hunting.

So he leapt out of bed with his customary vigour, anticipating the delights of the breakfast chafing dishes downstairs. He remembered his mother's old adage: stuff a cold and starve a fever. Time for him to get stuffing. But then he stopped. An idea was burgeoning in his brain.

From long experience, he gave it time to burgeon. Ideas never flashed into Blotto's brain; they glowed there slowly under a lot of clinker.

But when this one finally did burst into flame, he had to admit it was a real buzzbanger. He had a cold—what a spoffing great gift! He would do what other people did in that situation. He would announce that he was indisposed and therefore could not go hunting.

But he'd do it cunningly. If he broke the news too early, Laetitia Melmont might seize the opportunity to make a similar announcement, though without the excuse of a cold. And he'd have to spend the whole day with her chasing him around the corridors of Snitterings.

So he dressed in hunting gear and duly went downstairs to stuff his cold. Kedgeree, bacon, sausages, kidneys, scrambled eggs, toast and marmalade—he ate the lot. And fortunately his presence at the breakfast table didn't coincide with Laetitia's. Though he did have to suffer further puerile braying from the Duke's Old Harrovians.

Still, it wasn't going to be for long. Though they didn't possess the nuanced skills required by cricket, they all liked the simpler pleasures of seeing animals killed, so they were all going off hunting. The solitary day ahead of him became even more attractive.

As he left the breakfast room he met his sister, splendid in her *tenue de chasse*. A day spent in the field with such a breath-sapper was going to make the Duke's cronies drool even more.

'Twinks,' Blotto whispered urgently, 'I'm going to cut the hunting.'

'Really?' She had never expected to hear those words issue from her brother's lips.

'Suffering from a heavy cold. Not to mention rather a surfeit of the Laetitias.'

'Ah.' Twinks understood perfectly. 'So why are you dressed like that?'

'Part of a plan,' he confided. His sister waited in trepidation. The track record of Blotto's 'plans' was not without blemish. In fact, it was solid blemish from one wall to the other.

'If Laetitia were to see me in mufti, she'd get a whiff that the Stilton's iffy. So I've togged myself up and I'm going to wait till everyone else is mounted before the "Yoicks Tallyho!" Then I'll make my announcement.'

'But—'

'And I want you to help me, Twinks, me old bloater.'

'How?'

'Engage Laetitia in conversation when she's up on her nag. Ride off with her. Charm her with your chittle-chattle. Don't let her notice that I'm hors d'oeuvre.'

Twinks looked puzzled for a moment, then said gently, 'I think you mean *hors de combat*, Blotto.'

'Oh yes, right, whatever. Anyway, will you do that for me?'

'Of course, Blotto. Don't you worry, it'll all be creamy éclair.'

And it was. Twinks, as ever, played her role to perfection, and Blotto timed his announcement with comparable skill. Snitterings felt wonderfully empty after the hunting party had thundered away. The only above stairs people left were Blotto and the two Dowager Duchesses. The Dowager Duchess of Melmont was too infirm to go hunting, and the Dowager Duchess of Tawcester was still suffering from a slow-healing broken hip which necessitated the use of a walking stick. So the two of them also stayed in the house, relishing the prospect of trading further insults.

When Blotto got back to his room after the hunting party had set off, he couldn't believe how easy his escape had been. He moved across to the window, feeling a wonderful air of freedom. The hunters could be out for as much as eight hours. At least four, anyway. Four hours without the threat of Laetitia Melmont—there was a God, even if you were only Church of England.

He looked down to the Snitterings garages. Outside one Corky Froggett was labouring to add yet another layer of shine to the already perfect bodywork of the Tawcester Towers Rolls-Royce. The chauffeur had taken off his jacket and was working in shirtsleeves and braces though, given his upright bearing, Corky still looked as if he were in uniform. He caught his master's eye and waved up cheerily. Blotto returned the salutation and moved away from the window.

He felt rather good lying in his bed. The sheets weren't so clammy in the daytime. He'd changed back into his pyjamas because that's what he believed people who gave in to colds did.

And he'd taken the precaution of asking the Snitterings butler Proops to send up a bottle of whisky and a soda syphon. He knew people recommended whisky to dry up colds. Autumn sun washed through the window over his coverlet. The day stretched pleasurably ahead of him.

In such a situation some people might have suffered from boredom, might have felt the need to read a book or do a crossword puzzle. Not Blotto. Though *The Hand of Fu Manchu* was there on his bedside table, the effort of reading even that—he never did more than a page at a time anyway—seemed insuperable. He was content just to lie there, to let vacancy expand and fill up his mind.

His happy reverie was broken by the sound of a tap on the door. Before he had time to grant permission, it opened to reveal Laetitia Melmont, looking even bigger in her hunting gear.

'Hello, Blotto,' she said, as she strode across to entrench herself on the side of his bed. 'I heard you're ill, and, just like Florence Nightingale, I've come to minister to you.'

Chapter Three

A Compromising Situation

Blotto felt as awkward as an Anglican in the Vatican. He may not have known much about women, but he knew that the stakes in his potential connection to Laetitia had suddenly just soared into the stratosphere. She was in his bedroom! An actual live, breathing woman was in the bedroom of the Honourable Devereux Lyminster! If anyone ever found out about that, he wouldn't be thought Honourable at all. He'd be ruined. Matrimony would be the only possible way out.

But Blotto really didn't want to get married—and certainly not to 'the Snitterings Ironing-Board'. This was a gluepot deeper than any of the previous ones whose depths he had plumbed. He had somehow to get her out of his bedroom before anyone saw her there.

Or heard her there. As Blotto knew too well, Laetitia had one of those voices that can talk to relatives in the Colonies without the intervention of a telephone. Murmured sweet nothings from her sounded like the shouts of shipwrecked sailors. And murmured sweet nothings were, unfortunately, the mode of speech she seemed to be favouring that morning.

'Blotto,' she said in a little girl voice (which didn't suit her, because whatever Laetitia Melmont may once have been, she was no longer a little girl), 'you are so chivalrous.'

'Er?'

'Not telling me you are unwell, slipping away quietly, not wanting your illness to spoil my day's hunting.'

'Um...'

'But when I heard you had a bad cold, of course I had to rush back here to look after you.'

'Who told you I had a bad cold?' Surely Twinks wouldn't have sold her brother down the plughole?

'It was one of the Duke's friends.' Oh well, typical of that bunch to ruin a day that was going perfectly swimmingly.

'Tell me,' Laetitia went on, 'do you feel really ill?'

Blotto hesitated. His first instinct was to laugh off the idea. He'd only got a cold, after all. But then the thought came to him that serious illness might have something going for it.

'Oh, I'm sure I'll pull through.' The bravery in his voice was let down by a bout of feeble coughing, which he allowed to mutate into a gasping wheeze. 'If only I could breathe. That's the sty in the eye when it comes to life, isn't it? We keep needing to breathe. If we didn't have to do that, everything'd be all tickey-tockey, wouldn't it?'

'And are you having difficulty breathing, Blotto?'

'Well, a bit, yes.'

'Are you sure,' asked Laetitia coquettishly (and 'coquettish' suited her precisely as well as 'winsome' did), 'you are not having difficulty breathing because I am so close to you?'

'Good Lord, no. I can put you right on that. It is just the cold,' was Blotto's less than gallant reply. But now she mentioned it, he noticed that Laetitia had got considerably closer to him. From sitting on the edge of the bed she seemed imperceptibly to have shifted to being draped over him like an extra counterpane.

Then he had a brainwave. 'Actually, I wouldn't get too close to me if I were you, Laetitia.'

'Why ever not?'

'Because this illness I've got is very infectious.'

'How do you know?'

That stumped him. But only for a second. Then in a moment of brilliant improvisation he replied, 'I know, because just before you came into my room I noticed a spider crawling across my pillow...and I breathed on it...and it immediately shrivelled up and died. And I really wouldn't want you to shrivel up and die, Laetitia.' It was true. He certainly wanted the girl out of his life, but he didn't wish her any harm. Not of the shrivelling up and dying sort, anyway.

'Wouldn't it be rather wonderful,' Laetitia Melmont trilled loudly, 'to die of an illness one had caught from the man one loves?'

'No, it'd be a total waste of gingerbread,' said Blotto. 'Bad enough the boddo dying but there's no need for the filly who loves him to...' He was silent for a moment while he mentally recapitulated Laetitia's last speech. Then tentatively he asked, 'What is this about "the man one loves"? Who, for example is "one" in this instance?'

'I am "one",' Laetitia Melmont replied dramatically. 'Oh, you foolish boy, Blotto. Haven't you realized yet that I love you?'

'Well...I...erm...'

'Is it because you are too humble, Blotto? Is it because you do not think you are worthy of me?'

Sensing a possible escape route, he concurred: 'Yes, that's the right ticket. Not worthy of you. Totally wrong. If we got together, I'd just bring you down to my own pathetic level.'

'No!' came the magnificent reply. 'I would raise you to my level, Blotto. I would make something of you.'

'But I'm quite happy with what I'm currently made of, thank you.'

'Don't be so unambitious!'

'I mean, look, Laetitia, I'm just an ordinary old pineapple like—'

'Don't worry, your lack of intelligence will not interfere with the plans I have for you.'

'And I'm not interested in anything except hunting and cricket.'

'I will regard it as my duty to inculcate you in the mysteries of the Arts.'

'The Arts?' Blotto echoed miserably. Once again he sought the security of his illness. 'It's very kind of you, Laetitia,' he said in a frail voice, his eyes fluttering almost to closure, 'and I do appreciate you making all these plans for me...but they may all be in vain...I really am not feeling at all well...in fact, I wonder whether I will last the day...' He knew this was laying it on with a butter knife, but he was working towards a new solution that had just come to him. 'In fact, I think it would be best if I were to get Corky Froggett, our chauffeur, to drive me back to Tawcester Towers as soon as possible. I would like to spend my last hours in those beautiful sylvan surroundings that I know so well.'

'Blotto,' Laetitia Melmont announced seriously, 'if you are really dying...'

'Well, it does feel that way at the moment.' He was pleased she seemed to be accepting the idea so readily.

'If you are really dying,' she repeated, 'it would be terrible for you to go to your grave without the real love of a woman.'

'Oh, it's been all right,' said Blotto airily. 'My sister Twinks loves me. And I think the old Mater does...in her way.'

'When I said "the real love of a woman", I meant not the love of Agape, but the love of Eros.'

'I'm afraid I don't know the chaps you're referring to...' The words drained from Blotto's mouth. He may not have known the individuals concerned, but suddenly he did understand what Laetitia was talking about. And to leave him in no doubt that he'd finally got the point, he observed that she was starting to undo the buttons of her hunting jacket.

Oh, broken biscuits. Religion did not play much of a part in Blotto's life—he was Church of England, after all—but in this terrible extremity he found himself praying to someone or something to get him out of it.

And that someone or something was clearly a benign divinity. Before Laetitia had reached the lowest button of her jacket, they were both frozen by the sound of a terrible scream issuing from the garden below.

Not even pausing to cover his pyjamas with the decency of a dressing gown, Blotto sprang to the window and looked down.

In the middle of the kitchen garden, spread-eagled on her front in a recently raked bed where the four brick paths met, lay the Dowager Duchess of Melmont. She had been impaled by a pitchfork.

Blotto felt a little guilty. When in future he used prayers to someone or something to get him out of a gluepot, he'd try to do so with a little more discretion. It was as though he had actually prayed for a murder. A considerably less radical distraction to deter Laetitia from disrobing would have done the job. But he couldn't stop himself from feeling huge relief that the ploy had worked.

Chapter Four

The Body in the Kitchen Garden

'Go to your room immediately!' Blotto commanded Laetitia, who had yet to see the ghastliness that lay below.

'But—'

'Go to your room! A crisis has occurred at Snitterings, and dealing with it is going to be man's work.'

'Oh, Blotto,' Laetitia simpered, 'I do love it when you're masterful.'

That word 'love' again. But he was too preoccupied to worry about it. And at least Laetitia did as she was told and went to her room.

As, throwing on dressing gown and slippers, he hurtled along the corridor, Blotto just had time to register that he'd had a very narrow escape, he'd been a mere batsqueak away from disaster. Hoopee-doopee, no one actually knew that Laetitia had been in his bedroom. He wouldn't have to marry her after all.

Rushing down the creaking back stairs, he reached the kitchen garden in a matter of seconds. He was the first person there except for the now hysterical tweeny who had discovered the Dowager Duchess of Melmont's body and whose scream had saved Blotto's chitterlings. As he moved towards the corpse, other servants began to emerge from the house. Seeing that there was someone from 'above stairs' on the scene, they hovered together on the periphery of the action. It wasn't their place to take any initiative when there was a toff around.

Blotto looked down at the body. There was no doubt that the Dowager Duchess was dead. Nobody had a pitchfork with eighteen-inch tines shoved through them and survived. There was surprisingly little blood visible staining the lilac silk georgette of her dress at the back, but small rivulets of red trickled out from under her body on to the raked earth of the vegetable patch.

But that was not the only red at the scene. On the dome of the Dowager Duchess of Melmont's dowager's hump was the imprint of a crimson hand!

Blotto was about to crouch for a closer look at the body when he heard a familiar voice behind him and turned to greet his mother.

The Dowager Duchess of Tawcester looked down at her rival with contempt. 'Absolutely typical of Pansy. I get a broken hip, so, not to be outdone, she has to go and have this visited on her.'

And she stumped off back towards the house, as fast as her broken hip and walking stick would allow. As she approached the back door, Proops the Snitterings butler intercepted her with appropriate deference. One Dowager Duchess was dead, so he turned immediately to the other for instructions. From long experience, it never occurred to him for a moment that the Duke might have anything useful to contribute to the situation.

'Your Grace,' he intoned, 'is it your wish that the police should be summoned to investigate this crime?'

'Oh, I suppose they'll have to be,' the Dowager Duchess of Tawcester replied pettishly. 'It's not as if it's just a servant who's been murdered. I suggest that you telephone Inspector Trumbull.'

'Inspector Trumbull? I am not familiar with him, Your Grace. I don't believe there is anyone of that name in the Melmontshire Constabulary.'

'No, of course there isn't. Inspector Trumbull's from the Tawcestershire Constabulary.'

'I believe it is the normal custom, Your Grace,' Proops hazarded, 'for the initial investigation into a murder to be undertaken by the police force from the area closest to—'

'Any murder I'm involved in,' the Dowager Duchess boomed, 'is investigated by Inspector Trumbull and Sergeant Knatchbull of the Tawcestershire Constabulary! They understand their role in such proceedings and can be relied upon to be permanently baffled. Telephone them immediately!'

The Snitterings butler bowed. 'Very good, Your Grace.' And he watched her totter majestically into the house. Proops then, in the precise same tone with which the Dowager Duchess of Tawcester had diminished him, ordered his staff to stop gawping and get back to their work. Leaving Blotto alone in the kitchen garden.

He looked more closely at the handprint on the Dowager's hump, and noticed something strange. Its red was different from the colour of the blood that still ran and eddied from beneath the corpse. He sniffed close to the dead Dowager's back. There was no doubt about it. The mark of the crimson hand had been made in paint.

'What's the bizz-buzz, Blotto? Another corpse, I gather?'

He turned with relief—as he had so many times before—at the sound of his sister's voice. Now Twinks was on the scene, everything would be all right.

'I thought you were out making life difficult for the foxes,' he said in puzzlement. She was still dressed in her *tenue de chasse*.

'Yes, I was. But when I saw Laetitia had slipped the collar, I came back to rescue you from her grasping talons.'

'You're the absolute top of the milk, Twinks.'

'When I know my brother's in danger, I come flying to the rescue like a hare on roller skates. Tell me, did Laetitia find you?' Blotto's Adam's apple bobbled awkwardly in his throat. Pity filled his sister's azure eyes. 'Tough Gorgonzola, me old bull's-eye. But you managed to evade the deadly tentacles?'

A pallor crossed Blotto's face as he twigged just how close he had come to disaster. 'Only just,' he croaked. 'If there hadn't been a scream from the pipsqueak who found this body...' The full awfulness of what might have happened drained the words from his mouth.

'Anyway, talking of the body,' said Twinks, taking a look at it, 'tough rusk for the old Dowager Duchess, but...it's an investigation, isn't it? Grandissimo, what?'

A glow suffused not only Blotto's face, but his entire body. He hadn't really registered the investigative aspect of the murder. Twinks was always quicker at spotting stuff like that. But now he realized the two of them actually had a case to solve. For the first time his weekend at Snitterings offered a chink of sunlight through the curtains.

He watched with appropriate deference as his sister inspected the crime scene. There was an established demarcation of duties in all their investigations. Anything that involved derring-do, reckless bravery or physical confrontation—that was Blotto's half of the Camembert. Anything that involved observation, deductive skill...in a word, brainwork...then Twinks took up the baton.

She started with a close examination of the body. Aware of the basic rules of Scene of Crime procedure, she did not touch the defunct Dowager Duchess, but she went as close as she dared, allowing all of her senses to make their observations.

'Well, the first thing that's obvious, Blotto me old sideboard, is that the old girl hasn't been dead long.' She didn't give him a chance to ask his customary 'How do you know that,

Twinks?', but went straight on. 'The blood flow's stopping now, but I'd say she was coffinated within the last half-hour. Which of course means...?' Again she didn't wait for her brother to supply an answer. Time was of the essence. 'It means that the stencher who did this can't have got far off the old prems, can he?'

'Or she,' said Blotto, knowing how much his sister believed in fair biddles amongst murderers of either gender.

'"Or she"—good ticket, Blotto.' He glowed in the beam of his sister's approbation. 'Now the other fruity crumb about this murder is that we've got a limited number of suspects.'

'Have we?' Blotto's glow was quickly extinguished. It never took long for him to get left behind when Twinks's brain was really sparking.

'Think about it. Where are most of the boddos who're staying at Snitterings this weekend?'

Blotto glowed again. 'Out hunting.'

'Top ticket, Blotto, you've won the coconut!'

'And it's also dashed convenient, because, with all our sort of people out in the field, it means this ghastly crime must've been committed by someone below stairs...which is always rather a relief.'

'Unless, of course, our old Mater did it.'

Blotto looked at his sister aghast. 'You don't really think—'

'Of course I don't, you Grade A poodle. I was only joking.' Relief flooded Blotto's countenance as Twinks went on: 'Because I was out with the tally-hoes, I know for a fact that the only person to leave the hunt and return to Snitterings was Laetitia Melmont. Now we know she didn't kill her mother...'

'Do we, though?' asked her brother. 'You read some pretty whiffy stuff in the Sunday papers about that sort of thing. Mothers and daughters can brush each other's fur the wrong way. Very deep rivalry, according to that German woodlouse Frood.'

'I think you mean Freud, Blotto. And he's Austrian.'

'Maybe, but—'

'Anyway, the reason we know Laetitia Melmont didn't kill her mother is that she has an alibi.'

'Does she?'

'She was with you, Blotto.' Twinks would never show anything as extreme as exasperation to her brother, but there was a slight edge in her voice.

'Oh yes.' He nodded blithely. But his reassurance was short-lived. 'Rodents, though, suppose that comes out in the course of the investigation...? I'll be in a real gluepot if we have to tell the world Laetitia was in my bedroom. I won't be able to avoid marrying her then, will I?'

A furrow spoiled his sister's perfect brow. 'No, you're right there, Blotto me old cabbage. That would be a real rat in the larder.' But Twinks was never cast down for long. She could always find a solution to every problem. 'Don't go and pull on your worry-boots, though. We'll see to it that Laetitia's whereabouts are kept under the dustbin lid. And the best way to do that is to find out who actually killed the Dowager Duchess. When we can announce that little detail, nobody'll give a half-slice of burnt toast for other people's alibis.'

'Good ticket,' said Blotto, relieved. 'So who do you think did it, Twinks me old biscuit barrel?'

'Well, I'm not quite in the home straight yet, but I'm sure it won't take me long to string the flag up.' Her eyes moved back to the dead Dowager Duchess. 'Now I must really concentrate on this...'

Blotto was, as ever, reverently silent while he watched his sister's clue-gathering. Even in her *tenue de chasse* she carried her reticule, in which, amongst many other things, was her basic Scene of Crime kit. A magnifying glass, a miniature camera, a tape measure, tweezers, cotton wool and a pack of small brown envelopes to put the evidence in.

Twinks started with the raked earth of the vegetable bed in which the Dowager Duchess of Melmont lay. She inspected the scuffled marks near the edge with her magnifying glass and took a couple of photographs. She measured the length of the pitchfork handle and its angle to the horizontal. Then she went across to the far side of the bed and showed interest in some very small scratch-marks. Satisfied with what she had found there, she next inspected the four brick paths that radiated out from the central bed, paying particular attention to the one that led back to the house. Every now and then she would crouch down to scrutinize something with her magnifying glass before photographing what she had found.

Eventually she stopped by the arched doorway of the kitchen garden. 'Blotto me old trouser button, I think I'm getting somewhere.'

'You know who did it?' her brother asked eagerly.

Twinks raised a delicate hand in a gesture of remonstrance. 'Don't bash before the bully-off, Blotto. Give me a chance. But what I do know is that whoever coffinated the Dowager Duchess, he—or she—came in through this archway and left by the same route.'

'Ah.' Blotto tried to keep disappointment out of his voice. He really had hoped for a bit more from his sister's deductive skills. 'What I want to know,' he went on, 'is why the victim was here in the first place. Dowager Duchesses don't normally frequent kitchen gardens, do they?'

'Well, that I can answer for you,' said Twinks. 'Come and have a look at this.' She led her brother to the far side of the vegetable bed and pointed down to the scratch-marks in the raked soil. 'What do you make of those, Blotto?'

'Some small animal?' he conjectured. 'A rabbit?'

'No, rabbit's feet have five toes. The marks here show four pads and four nails.'

'Do they? Toad-in-the-hole!' murmured Blotto, uncertain.

'Which means they are marks left by a dog. Now who's got a dog here at Snitterings?'

The clouds cleared from his brow. 'The Dowager Duchess! That ghastly little reptile called Clutterbuck. I see. So the old fruitcake decided to take her dog for a walk in the kitchen garden.'

'No, she never walks the dog. She always carries it. Anyway, if you take a look at these marks in the soil, the Peke appears to have been dragged along.'

'What does that mean?'

'It means, Blotto, that Clutterbuck was seized from the Dowager Duchess, put on a lead and dragged down here.'

'But why would anyone want to do that?'

'Because the old vulture loved that dog like a pike loves troutlings. If Clutterbuck was taken away from her, she'd go anywhere to find him. Even into the kitchen garden.'

'Where her murderer awaited her.'

'Give that pony a rosette!'

'So who actually—?'

But before Blotto could reiterate the whole whodunit question, Twinks had grabbed him by the hand and was leading him away from the corpse. 'For the next part of our investigation, me old trombone, we need to go to the house and outbuildings. Ah, look!'

She pointed to the path in front of them. A tiny dot of crimson showed on the duller red of the bricks. 'Paint, Blotto me old gumdrop! A drop of paint or I'm an Apache Dancer! The coffinator came this way!'

Chapter Five

Twinks Points the Finger

There were a few other drops of red paint outside the kitchen garden, and Twinks, with Blotto in tow, had no difficulty in following them across to the Snitterings outbuildings at the back of the house. Half of the old stables had been converted into garages. In one of them the Tawcester Towers Rolls-Royce gleamed from Corky Froggett's ministrations. Of the chauffeur himself there was no sign, though his black jacket still hung from a nail on the garage door-frame, so he couldn't be that far away.

Since the majority of the weekend guests were off hunting, almost all of the Snitterings cars were in their allocated places. There was the usual mix of Rolls-Royces, Bentleys and Hispano-Suizas, as well as a handful of shooting brakes. Only the garage next door to the Snitterings Rolls-Royce was empty.

And it was there that the trail of paint spots led.

Twinks stopped to examine the tyre tracks leading away from the garage. 'I'd put my last shred of laddered silk stocking on the fact that the vehicle which has driven out of here is an old Napier shooting brake. From the depth of the indentations, I'd say there was only one person in it...and from the dust that has settled back into the tracks he didn't leave more than an hour and seventeen minutes ago.'

Blotto listened to his sister with his customary blank admiration. Then she leapt forward to rootle around in the dusty clutter at the back of the garage.

'What are you looking for, old pineapple?' he asked, as he moved across to make faces at himself in the chrome of the Rolls-Royce that gleamed from Corky Froggett's polishing. Then he noticed a couple of unusual objects lying on the floor by the car. He picked up the one that looked like an oversized sink-plunger, and scrutinized it.

'I'm looking for whatever it was that the murdy coffinator was carrying that dripped red paint,' his sister replied.

'Any idea what kind of thing it might be?'

'If I'm right, it's a kind of large rubber stamp in the shape of a hand.'

'Like this?' asked Blotto, appearing round the corner of the empty garage door.

Twinks looked up from her dusty searches. 'Exactly like that!' She inspected the object that Blotto held out to her. At the end of a three-foot wooden handle was a metal disc, to which was glued the outline of a hand. Its rubber showed traces of red paint. 'Now all we need to find is the ink-pad—or perhaps I should say the paint-pad—that the stencher used to prime the thing.'

'Oh, I think I could show you that too.' Nonchalantly, enjoying the rare experience of taking the lead in one of their investigations, Blotto ushered his sister to the adjacent garage. With pride, he pointed down to a shallow metal dish containing a couple of inches of red paint.

'Splendissimo!' shrieked Twinks, and her brother felt positively fizzulated.

Then he noticed that, presumably when the dish had been placed down on the floor, a tiny amount of red paint had splashed up on to the Rolls-Royce's back mudguard. 'Corky's going to be pretty vinegared off about that,' he observed. He took a handkerchief out of his pocket and went across to wipe off the droplet. But it had already set hard. 'He'll be more than vinegared off. He'll be absolutely fumacious about it.'

Their attention was drawn to the sound of muffled yapping. Leaping up on the back seat of the Rolls-Royce and only intermittently visible due to his size, a very disgruntled Clutterbuck was assaulting the window. Round his neck was an improvised lead of coarse rope.

'We'd better let the little slug out, I suppose,' said Twinks. When Blotto had effected that, she continued, 'We'll take him indoors, then Proops can find someone to look after him.'

'Tickey-tockey!' As Blotto took a firm hold on the dog's rope, he was rewarded by a meaty bite into his ankle, exposed between pyjama and bedroom slipper. 'You little...Harrovian!' he hissed, unable to think of a worse insult.

Below stairs there was a marked reluctance to take over the guardianship of Clutterbuck. It became clear that he was generally loathed, and the staff found much riper and less decorous descriptions of the creature than Blotto had. While the Dowager Duchess of Melmont had been alive, they'd had to keep their opinions to themselves. With their mistress out of the way, they showed no such inhibitions. Eventually Proops delegated a housemaid who'd recently allowed her feather duster to knock over a priceless Ming vase to look after the dog. It was part of her punishment.

With that task completed, the butler led Blotto and Twinks into his pantry. 'You said you wished to ask me some questions, milady.'

'Yes, Proops. It's about the murder of the Dowager Duchess.'

'Really? Well, I don't believe there is anything else that needs to be done at this juncture. All customary procedures have been followed. Your mother has called in her own police investigators from Tawcestershire...'

'Inspector Trumbull and Sergeant Knatchbull,' Blotto supplied.

'Those were the names she mentioned, yes, milord. So the proper authorities have been informed about the crime. All we have to do is wait. Though I would assume that, long before the police have arrived, the case will have been solved by the know-it-all amateur sleuth, Mr Troubadour Bligh, who is conveniently staying here at Snitterings for the weekend. That is what usually happens.'

'Ah, but suppose there were another know-it-all amateur sleuth staying here at Snitterings for the weekend...?'

Twinks twinkled her azure eyes at Proops. Though trained as a butler never to show more extreme reaction to anything than a phlegmatically raised eyebrow, he was no more immune to her charms than the rest of his gender. 'And who might that person be?' he asked haltingly.

'Little me,' replied Twinks. 'And to complete my investigation, I do need a bit of information from you, Proops.'

The butler was patently thrilled by the intimate use of his surname. (He must once have had a first name, but in the course of long service even he had forgotten it). A tremor ran through both of his eyebrows at the same time.

'Anything I can do to help, milady.'

'Do you know precisely where all your staff are at this moment, Proops?'

'My own staff, yes. I cannot account for all the grooms and coachmen, who are probably with the hunting party. Nor the gardeners, though presumably they're off gardening somewhere. Anyway, such people answer to the estate manager, not me. Of my own "below stairs" staff, however, I can account for every one.'

'So if I asked you to find any single member of your staff, you could do it immediately?'

'A matter of moments, milady.'

'I am looking,' Twinks trilled, fully aware of the effect she was having on the butler, 'for a young man of about six foot four inches in height. He has dark hair which he wears rather longer than most young men, and he walks with a slight limp, probably due to a recent injury to his left foot.'

'There is only one member of my staff who fits that description, milady. One of the younger footmen. His name is Will Tyler.'

'Would it be possible for you to bring him here to talk to me?' Twinks cooed.

'Of course. As I say, a matter of moments, milady.' And the butler bustled out of his pantry, as determined as any knight errant to do doughty deeds for his damsel.

'Well, Twinks,' observed Blotto, 'that's another man you've got dangling on your charm bracelet.'

His sister giggled. She didn't even bother to make the giggle self-deprecating. Having vacuumed the breath out of so many of them, she knew the power she had over men.

'Incidentally,' Blotto went on, 'how did you know all that stuff about the stencher who coffinated the Dowager Duchess? Did you actually see the running sore in action?'

'No, of course not. I deduced it.'

'How?'

'It was terribly simple. The angle that the pitchfork was shoved into the old fruitcake's back told me how tall he was. Stuck on the rope he'd used as a lead for Clutterbuck was a long dark hair which smelled of that nasty cheap brilliantine favoured by the oikish classes. And the uneven footprints on the edge of the vegetable bed told me about his foot injury. Whole thing was easy as a housemaid's virtue, Blotters.'

Her brother blushed. Twinks could be quite racy at times. But his embarrassment was short-lived, as a very concerned-looking Proops bustled into his pantry, followed by an equally concerned-looking housekeeper.

'Will Tyler is not on the premises,' the butler announced.

'No,' said Twinks coolly. 'He left Snitterings...' She consulted her watch. '...an hour and fifty-three minutes ago. Driving an old Napier shooting brake.'

'But why would he do that, milady?'

'Because...' She paused for maximum effect. '...Will Tyler had just murdered the Dowager Duchess of Melmont.'

Even though there was no perpetrator present to point at, Twinks's finger moved up by habit into an accusatory position.

Chapter Six

A Denouement in the Library

And because he entered Proops's pantry at that precise moment, Troubadour Bligh found that Twinks's finger was pointing at him. 'Ooh, what do you think I've done wrong then, you little minx?' he asked in his shrill feminine voice.

Now Blotto didn't normally stand on ceremony. He was the last person to bother about whether anyone called him 'milord' or not. But he did find his bristles bristling at a common know-it-all polymathic amateur sleuth calling his sister a 'little minx'. Bligh certainly didn't know her well enough to exercise that kind of familiarity. Blotto was about to remonstrate, but then he caught the negative instruction in his sister's eye.

'I doubt that you have done anything wrong, Mr Bligh,' said Twinks.

'I wouldn't be too sure about that,' the know-it-all polymathic amateur sleuth responded archly. 'Anyway, I'm here on important business. The Dowager Duchess has been murdered, and I'm about to deduce whodunit. I don't come on country house weekend parties just for the fun of it, you know.'

'Well, actually you're a bit late on the deducing whodunit routine, because...' Again Blotto caught his sister's eye and his words trickled away.

'I don't think this one'll take long,' Troubadour Bligh announced confidently. 'Proops, have the hunting party returned yet?'

'Not quite, but I can hear their horns approaching. I would have thought they would be back in the house within the next half-hour, sir.'

'Very good. That gives me plenty of time to conduct my investigation.' The know-it-all polymathic amateur sleuth consulted the watch that dangled rather foppishly from a chain in his waistcoat pocket. 'Would you see to it that all the guests are assembled in the library at six o'clock this evening?'

The butler inclined his head. 'Of course, sir.'

'And,' Troubadour Bligh continued grandly, 'could you see that all of the below stairs staff are also there as well?'

Proops could not prevent an indrawn breath before replying evenly, 'Of course, sir.' He knew that a lot of the below stairs staff had never ventured into that aristocratic sanctum. Most of them wouldn't have recognized a library if it had jumped up and bitten them on the shin.

Blotto had been at enough of these everyone-gathered-in-the-library occasions at country house weekends to know the form. Even when Twinks, something of an innovator in such time-honoured routines, was the amateur sleuth doing the finger-pointing, she still started with the traditional formula of words.

And so, sure enough, did Troubadour Bligh. 'You may be wondering why I've asked you here...' he began.

Since everyone present knew the answer, no one bothered to respond. They made up a strange party. Except in the event of a patronizing moment at Christmas or a house fire, 'above stairs' and 'below stairs' never mixed like this, and the two factions regarded each other with considerable suspicion. There was no intermingling of them in the library. On one side sat the toffs, on the other stood the common people.

Needless to say, seated in a leather-covered throne-like chair, Blotto and Twinks's mother was in charge of proceedings. With one Dowager Duchess permanently off the scene, it was naturally assumed that another of that doughty breed would take over the reins. Again no one considered for a moment the possibility of the Duke of Melmont having any role in the proceedings.

He stood, looking rather uncomfortable, surrounded by his Old Harrovian chums. Neither he nor his sister Laetitia had shown any evidence of grief at their mother's demise. Whether this was because their upper lips had been stiffened rigid by their upbringing, or because neither of them had ever liked the old fruitbat, was impossible to judge.

Some of the younger members of the below stairs contingent—tweenies, scullery maids and so on—were awestruck by their unfamiliar surroundings. They looked with bewilderment at the shelves which covered all of the room's walls, wondering what on earth all those leather-bound objects on them were. Some of the Duke's Old Harrovians demonstrated the same ignorance.

Grinning across at Corky Froggett, who stood, as ever, at attention in his black uniform, Blotto observed that there was someone else trying to catch the chauffeur's eye. One of the cooks, a splendidly upholstered woman in her early thirties, seemed anxious to make eye contact, but Corky studiously avoided her gaze.

Blotto did not, however, have time to think further about this oddity as Troubadour Bligh, clapping his hands effetely for attention, said, 'Your Grace, Your Other Grace, Milord, Milady,

Ladies, Gentlemen and Members of the Lower Orders, we are here in this library following the mean and cowardly murder of the Dowager Duchess of Melmont. The crime is rendered all the more despicable by the fact that it took place here at Snitterings, the Dowager Duchess's own home, where she was entertaining a party of her friends and equals for the weekend.

'Now the nature of the offence is such that no one could imagine that it could have been committed by a member of the upper classes, and fortunately in this case all of the people who fit that description are excluded from suspicion by the fact that they were out hunting at the time the murder took place. They all have alibis.' He looked around the library. 'I am correct in making that assumption, am I not?'

Blotto felt he had to say something. 'Erm, in fact I hadn't joined the other boddos out in the field. Laid up with a bit of a cold, don't you know?'

'Very good, milord,' said Troubadour Bligh. 'And you were in fact the first person to discover the body.'

'Well, one of the tweenies—'

'I did say "person", milord. I don't believe that tweenies come within the definition of that word.'

'No, of course not.'

'So, milord, you were the only member of the weekend party to stay here while everyone else went hunting?'

'Well...' Blotto, naturally as straight as a billiard cue, was about to mention Laetitia's presence in the house at the relevant time, but he caught a fierce look from his sister's azure eyes and thought better of the idea.

'So...' Troubadour Bligh's gaze moved firmly towards the standing side of the library. '...we are in no doubt that the murder was committed by someone "below stairs", an assumption we can readily make because there is only one other group of people who might commit such a crime, and I am delighted to say that we have no foreigners staying at Snitterings this weekend. Though of course that is a slightly unusual circumstance. At most house parties where I am called upon to exercise my amateur sleuthing skills there is at least one unsavoury person of un-British extraction—and normally with a guilty secret in his past.

'Be that as it may, the question now demands to be answered: which member of the domestic staff had the temerity to kill their noble benefactress? I have checked the scene of the crime for evidence and—'

'As a matter of fact,' Twinks interrupted coolly, 'we can cut through all this wiffle-waffle. I do actually know who—'

'Honoria!' Her mother's use of her proper name silenced Twinks instantly. 'It is not generally thought good form for members of our class to interrupt the summings-up of common little know-it-all polymathic amateur sleuths in the library.'

'I beg your pardon, Mater,' said Twinks, appropriately subdued.

'You may continue, Mr Bligh,' the Dowager Duchess announced.

'Thank you, Your Grace.' The little man stood between the two social factions, giving each the benefit of his deductive wisdom. 'As I said, I have checked the scene of this appalling crime and I have found conclusive evidence which will enable me to point a finger at the evil perpetrator.'

Blotto and Twinks exchanged looks. The temptation was strong for them both to burst into a unison cry of 'Will Tyler', but the look on their mother's face strangled that idea at birth.

'The Dowager Duchess of Melmont,' Troubadour Bligh continued, 'was killed by a single blow from a pitchfork driven into her back as she lay on her front on a raked-over vegetable bed in the kitchen garden.'

Oh, shift your shimmy, thought Blotto, we all know that.

But the know-it-all polymathic amateur sleuth was not going to be hurried. He had his own way of conducting his denouements and he wasn't about to change it for anyone.

'I examined the marks in the soil of the vegetable bed, and from that gathered a great deal of information about our murderer. Many questions were raised—questions which might not seem relevant to the average intellect, but whose pertinence was instantly recognized by my finely tuned investigative brain. The first question that seemed to me obvious to ask is why the Dowager Duchess should have been in the kitchen garden. It is not an area of the purlieus of Snitterings that she was in the habit of visiting.'

He then spelled out the way that the perpetrator had used Clutterbuck to lure his prey into such unfamiliar territory. Oh, put a jumping cracker under it, Twinks urged silently.

'Now the murderer, as I say,' Troubadour Bligh continued at his own pace, 'left marks in the soil of the vegetable bed which give an exact history of how the crime was committed. Those marks are as much a betrayal of his actions as if he had left fingerprints—or indeed a signed confession.

'From those traces I can tell the man's height and many other personal details. I have also been able to track down the device which he used to violate the late Dowager Duchess's body with the mark of a crimson hand. Minute droplets of the red paint he employed for that evil purpose led me to the instrument of desecration. It was not very well hidden.

'In fact, the murderer made a very poor job of covering his tracks. Not only did he allow paint to splash on the Rolls-Royce in which the party from Tawcester Towers were driven to Snitterings, he also used the car to imprison the late Dowager Duchess's Pekinese, Clutterbuck. Hairs from the dog are evident on the interior upholstery of the vehicle.

'All of which evidence makes the truth of what happened as clear to me as daylight. Our murderer, born into the lower orders of society, is clearly one of those misbegotten creatures who was never content with his station in life and who bore a lifelong resentment towards the upper classes. He is someone who has embraced the evil ideology of Socialism.'

A tremor ran through both factions in the Snitterings library at the mention of this disgusting concept.

'He is a man without moral scruples or any recognition of his appropriately humble position in society. He knows who he is, and all of you are about to share that knowledge. Unhesitatingly...' Troubadour Bligh raised his hand in anticipation of his customary final denouement gesture. '...I point my finger at the murderer of the Dowager Duchess of Melmont.'

With the instinct for timing which always brought them to the library just after an amateur sleuth had solved the crime, Inspector Trumbull and Sergeant Knatchbull then appeared. Following the direction in which Troubadour Bligh's finger was pointing, they immediately arrested Corky Froggett.

Chapter Seven

Wrongful Arrest

'I don't understand why you're making such a fuss,' the Dowager Duchess of Tawcester complained. 'It's not difficult to find another chauffeur.'

'That is not the point,' said Blotto, uncharacteristically argumentative to his mother. 'Corky's one in a million. He's as loyal as a spoffing spaniel.'

'What is more relevant,' Twinks added, 'is that he didn't commit the murder. He's been wrongfully arrested.'

The Dowager Duchess shrugged. True to her upbringing, she had never had much time for the concept of justice. If people of her class started asking themselves whether life was fair, they would be questioning the entire system of privilege from which they so benefited. So it was not an avenue to be explored. That the wrong person occasionally got imprisoned or hanged seemed to the Dowager Duchess part of the natural order of things. Nothing to get exercised about—particularly when the person in question was a member of the servant classes.

'I'm absolutely determined,' Twinks went on, 'that we get Corky free.'

'How on earth,' asked her mother, 'do you plan to do that?'

'By tracking down the real murderer and forcing a confession out of him.'

'And do you know who the real murderer is?'

'As a matter of fact, Mater, we do,' said Blotto. 'He's one of the Snitterings footmen called Will Tyler.'

The Dowager Duchess lost interest. If it was only another servant...

'What we need to do,' Twinks announced to her brother when the two of them were alone together, 'is to see Corky Froggett before he gets taken off to the Tawsworthy clink.'

Blotto looked dubious. 'I don't think Inspector Trumbull would be very keen on that idea.'

'Are you suggesting, me old cucumber sandwich, that I won't be able to get round Inspector Trumbull?'

Blotto knew his sister better than to say yes to that.

Corky Froggett had been locked in one of the Snitterings extensive range of cellars. Inspector Trumbull, having been neatly twisted round Twinks's little finger, unlocked the door for the sleuthing siblings. 'I shouldn't be doing this,' he announced. 'It very much goes against accepted police procedure. So I can only allow you to be with the prisoner for five minutes.'

'Half an hour,' Twinks corrected him.

'Very good, milady. But I will of course have to be present during your conversation.'

'No, you won't, Inspector.'

'Very good, milady.'

'You go to the kitchen and get yourself a cup of tea.'

'Very good, milady.' And Inspector Trumbull went off to do that.

Corky Froggett had been sitting on a chair in the single beam of autumn moonlight that straggled through the cellar's one-barred window, but he rose to his feet when he saw his visitors and stood in his customary position of attention.

'Good evening, milord, milady,' he said in a voice that appeared to have been born directly beneath Bow Bells.

'Well, this is a bit of a gluepot, isn't it?' observed Blotto.

'Don't worry about it, milord. I've been in stickier situations than this. I remember when I was in the trenches and the Hun sent out a raiding party armed to the teeth with—'

'But then,' Twinks interrupted, 'you had a chance of escape. Now you've been sewn up like a pin cushion, and there's a strong chance of your being hanged.'

'That's nothing for the likes of you to be concerned about, milady. I can take my punishment as well as the next man.'

'Yes, but, Corky,' said Blotto, 'it's a bit of a candle-snuffer for you to be taking punishment for something you didn't do.'

'That's just the way up the toast sometimes lands, milord. You can't go through life worrying about every little crack in the crock-pot.'

'I'd call being hanged more than a crack in the crock-pot,' said Twinks. 'Anyway, I'm delighted you're being so philosophical about being both feet in the quagmire, but we're determined to get you unarrested as quick as a lizard's lick.'

'That's very good of you, milady, but I don't think there's much chance. That little twinkle-twitterer Mr Bligh seems to have got a cast-iron case against me.'

'It may look like a cast-iron case, but the one thing it doesn't take into account is the fact that you didn't kill the Dowager Duchess, did you?'

'No, no, I certainly didn't.' Corky Froggett was affronted by the very suggestion. 'If I killed her you can tan my tongue and make it into a luggage strap.'

'Well, look, if you didn't do it,' reasoned Twinks, 'then there must be a way that we can prove you didn't do it.'

'What had you in mind, milady?'

'Let's say you had an alibi.'

'Ah.'

Corky Froggett's monosyllable was followed by a long silence. Then Blotto found himself in the unusual role of explainer. 'What my sister means is: Can you prove you were somewhere else at the moment when the murder of the Dowager Duchess was committed?'

'Um...'

'For instance,' Blotto suggested, 'were you with someone else at the time?'

Silence reasserted itself. Then Twinks had one of her brain-busting moments of intuition. 'I noticed in the library, Corky, that one of the Snitterings cooks was looking at you in a very special way.'

'"A very special way", milady?'

'Yes. Like a mother duck looks at one of her ducklings who dropped off the end of the line and then managed to catch up.'

This metaphor once again silenced the chauffeur.

'I have done some research below stairs, and I have discovered that the cook's name is Nancy. What I am suggesting, Corky, is that that was a *tendresse* between you and this cook Nancy...?' Enduring silence. 'That in fact, at the time of the Dowager Duchess's murder, you were in the company of this cook Nancy, snugly ensconced with her in the downstairs linen store?'

The expression on the chauffeur's face told her that she had won the coconut. But all he said was, 'If that were the case, milady, it is something I could not reveal, could I?'

'Why ever not?'

'Because, milady, to do so would impugn the honour of the lady involved.'

Blotto looked at his sister. 'Fair biddles, Twinks. Corky's right. No self-respecting boddo could do that, could he?'

'Sometimes,' Twinks observed, 'the concept of being a gentleman can be taken too far.'

She and her brother were sitting in the Snitterings library, empty now after the drama of Troubadour Bligh's accusations. Blotto looked puzzled. 'Sorry, not on the same page, me old biscuit barrel.'

'What I meant,' Twinks explained slowly, 'was that if Corky wasn't being such a gentleman, he could reveal that he'd been with Nancy at the time of the murder and get himself off the hook.'

'I can see that, but you have to admit that what he's doing is rather magnificent.'

'I don't think there's anything very magnificent about getting hanged for a crime you didn't commit.'

'No, but it still is the gentlemanly thing to do.'

'For the love of strawberries, Blotto! Corky Froggett isn't even a gentleman, so there's no need for him to be bound by the code of a gentleman.'

It was one of those very rare moments when his sister disappointed Blotto. 'Corky Froggett is one of nature's gentlemen,' he said quietly.

'Yes, yes.' A furrow of frustration formed on Twinks's perfect forehead. 'Well, all it means is that we've got to produce the real coffinator by express delivery. We must find Will Tyler.'

'And how do you propose setting about that?'

'First thing in the morning I will examine his living quarters with a pair of fine eyebrow tweezers. See if I can find any clues.'

'Shall I come and help?'

Twinks made her negative response as gracious as she could. Previous experience had told her that having Blotto with her on a clue-gathering mission was a bit like inviting a herd of buffalo. 'Anyway,' she went on, 'there's something else you need to do.'

'Oh? What's that? Come on, uncage the ferrets, old pineapple.'

'When we know where to look for Will Tyler, we're definitely going to need transport to track him down. Tomorrow morning you must go back to Tawcester Towers to pick up the Lagonda.'

A beatific smile settled on Blotto's face. He'd felt incomplete at Snitterings without his precious motor. Now he would be a whole man again. He thought, to fulfil himself totally, while he was at Tawcester Towers he might pick up his cricket bat too.

Chapter Eight

A Vile Conspiracy

The following morning Corky Froggett was taken in a Black Maria by Inspector Trumbull and Sergeant Knatchbull to Tawsworthy police station. Twinks saw the cook Nancy waving him off, and there was a tear in the woman's eye. For a moment Twinks contemplated confronting her, asking whether she would risk the hazard to her honour and supply the chauffeur with an alibi. But she remembered what her brother had said and restrained herself.

Blotto himself left soon after. Though the Black Maria was driving virtually past Tawcester Towers, it would have been unthinkable for the police officers to have offered a lift to someone of Blotto's breeding. So he was driven back home by one of the Snitterings chauffeurs in one of the Snitterings Rolls-Royces.

Though he was unaware of the fact, Blotto too was waved off by a woman with a tear in her eye. Laetitia

Melmont watched his departure from her bedroom window. Her match-making ambitions had been merely interrupted by her mother's death. She still had Blotto in her sights and was determined to bag him. And when Laetitia Melmont had her mind stuck on something, she demonstrated powers of adhesion that made limpets look apathetic. As the nuns at her convent school had discovered over the business of the Jam Roly-Poly.

For the next stage of her investigation Twinks once again sought out the Snitterings butler Proops. She found him in his pantry, a man at ease with himself. For a while the murder of the Dowager Duchess had threatened to disrupt the carefully regulated rhythms of the great house. Now that a perpetrator of the crime had been identified—even though it wasn't the real perpetrator of the crime—life could return to its unhurried normality.

Proops was therefore less than enthusiastic to discover that one of the house guests, Lady Honoria Lyminster, seemed to feel that there were still some aspects of the murder that required investigation. Of course it was not his place to argue with someone of her breeding, but butlerly resentment at what he was being asked to do showed in the slightest of muscular twitches at one corner of his mouth.

Her first request was a strange one. Did he by any chance have a photograph of Will Tyler? Proops was about to point out to the lady that people below stairs were not usually the subject of photographic portraiture, when he remembered that a picture had been taken of the entire staff when the King had visited Snitterings. He found a copy of the print and pointed out the perfidious footman. Twinks saw a tall young man with long hair and an expression of downtrodden resentment. She clicked her eyelids together twice like a camera shutter, and the image was indelibly printed on to her memory.

To Proops's annoyance, it turned out that that was not all this inconvenient house guest required. Acceding with bad grace to her second request, he summoned a footman to show the lady to the quarters formerly occupied by Will Tyler. This was an area of Snitterings into which someone like Twinks would not normally trespass. The staff accommodation, accessed by the back stairs, was a warren of attics and garrets, none of whose tiny rooms looked out over the front of the house.

As they climbed through the floors, Twinks tried to engage her guide in conversation. Unusually, her efforts went unrewarded. All she received for her pains were monosyllables which managed to keep only just the right side of civility. She was certainly not likely to glean any information about Will Tyler from his fellow footman.

He stopped by a door in the attic corridor and indicated that they had reached their destination. Announcing brusquely that, according to Proops's instructions, he would stay by the door during her researches, he let Twinks into the room.

The space was cramped, with unpapered wooden walls. It was more like an animal stall than a place for human habitation. For a fleeting moment Twinks began to consider that perhaps she ought to do more work with the poor. But the aberrant thought soon passed, and comforting aristocratic insensitivity reasserted itself.

The room's only furniture was a bed with a straw mattress and a broken-down chair. Which was just as well, because there wouldn't have been room for anything else. Hanging from a nail by the door was a spare footman's uniform, from which emanated the odour of ancient sweat.

The room looked, Twinks supposed, exactly as the room of a servant should look (it was one of the few subjects on which she wasn't an expert). There was only one discordant element in its decor. On a small shelf above the bed stood a row of books. Instinctively sensing their importance, Twinks moved across to examine them.

Their spines didn't make pretty reading for someone of her upbringing. Most of the bindings were red, and so were the contents. *Das Kapital. The Communist Manifesto.* Amongst these famous ones were other less familiar titles: *Fair Shares for All, Robespierre Was Right, An End to Privilege, Socialism for Boys* and *Off With Their Heads: The Plain Man's Guide to the Aristocracy.* Twinks wondered how the Dowager Duchess of Melmont had not known about the serpent she was nurturing in the bosom of her household. How dared Will Tyler display his works of pernicious ideology so openly? What an absolute stencher he must be.

But when she reflected, she realized how safe he had been. He could have filled his bedroom with bomb-making paraphernalia and none of his intended victims would have been any the wiser. His security was guaranteed by the huge divide there existed between below and above stairs.

Having checked out the books, Twinks turned her attention to the rest of the room, though with no great expectation of finding anything. Taking a deep breath, she drew back the grubby covers of the bed and lifted the mattress. Ends of straw escaping the stained ticking scratched at her elegant hands, but Twinks didn't allow that to hinder her search. Feeling along every inch of the mattress, she checked whether it had been used as a hiding place, but found nothing. She was about to replace the bedding when her eye caught a glimpse of a narrow cylinder protruding from the slats which would normally be covered by the mattress.

Twinks pulled the object from its cranny and scrutinized it. Though darkened and discoloured by much use, she could identify as ivory the foot-long stem to which what looked like a ceramic doorknob had been attached some three inches from the end. Seeing the hole in the top of this addition, Twinks knew immediately what the object she held was. And a sniff from her delicate nostrils confirmed instantly what the pipe has been used for.

Putting her find to one side, Twinks drew the bedding across the palliasse and turned to check through the pockets of

Will Tyler's noisome uniform. Her inspection revealed nothing but a torn scrap of paper on which someone had scrawled in pencil the words:

HAI
LEE'S.

Perhaps more significant, though, was what was printed across the top of the page. Though the tear had removed three of them, one finger and a thumb still remained. They came from the miniaturized imprint of a crimson hand.

Twinks realized that her investigation needed specialized assistance.

The County of Melmontshire abuts Oxfordshire and there was a good train service from the local station to the city of dreaming spires. Though she could easily have arranged for one of the Snitterings cars to take her all the way, Twinks decided to make most of the journey by the railway. She had often found that sitting anonymously in a compartment, listening to the rhythm of the train, freed her thoughts in a very constructive way.

There were plenty of taxicabs vying for business at Oxford station, but it was a brisk autumn day and Twinks decided she would walk to St Raphael's College. She liked the city and enjoyed the sight of book-laden undergraduates scuttling around in their flapping black gowns. She was so used to the reaction that she didn't notice the number of them who gawped, dropped their books or fell off their bicycles, dumbfounded by her beauty.

As she approached him, the porter at the main gate of St Raphael's gave Twinks a distinctly old-fashioned look. Although there had been what he thought of as 'undergraduettes' at Oxford for some decades, it had never been a development of which he approved. In his view, there was a place for women, and it certainly wasn't in universities. Under no circumstances was it in the all-male enclave of St Raphael's College. Least of all at eleven o'clock in the morning.

Twinks smiled at him in a way that she knew to be winsome, but then winsomeness had never failed her before. The porter, though, was made of strong misogynist stuff and he was in no mood to be charmed.

'The college is closed to visitors, miss,' he announced.

'Milady, in fact,' Twinks riposted. It wasn't her custom to stand on ceremony, but sometimes it was the only thing that people of the oikish classes understood.

'Very well, *milady*,' said the porter, 'but you still can't come in.'

'I have come to see Professor Erasmus Holofernes,' proclaimed Twinks.

The porter consulted some papers on his desk. 'I have no record here of Professor Holofernes expecting any visitors this morning. Therefore he cannot be expecting you.'

'No, of course he's not expecting me. But he'll be free to see me.'

'I would think that extremely unlikely, milady. The Professor works in his room all day. He never stirs from the college premises. His oak is permanently sported. Perhaps I should explain that expression, milady...?'

'Don't talk toffee. I know what it means. He closes his outer door to indicate that he doesn't want visitors.'

'Given that you know that, milady, I wonder why it ever occurred to you that the Professor might see you at this time of day. He does not see anyone while he is working...except the college servant who takes him his daily post.' The porter indicated a huge pile of letters, many of which bore stamps of foreign origin. 'The Professor works in total solitude until he joins his fellow dons for drinks at 6 p.m. in the Senior Common Room, followed by dinner in the Great Hall. And even then he doesn't see people of your...er, gender.'

'He'll see me. Use the telephone to inform him of my presence,' Twinks commanded.

Something in her voice, some atavistic intonation echoing centuries of mistreating the lower orders, had the desired effect. Cowed, the porter reached for the receiver. 'Who shall I say wishes to see the Professor, milady?'

'Twinks.'

'Twinks?' he echoed, scepticism returning to his voice. 'I cannot imagine that Professor Erasmus Holofernes includes in his acquaintances anyone by the name of "Twinks".'

'Will you please do your job, dial the relevant number and announce my presence to the Professor?' Twinks could at times sound dauntingly like her mother, and the porter did exactly as he was told.

To his astonishment he was immediately ordered by the voice at the other end of the telephone to direct Twinks to the rooms of Professor Erasmus Holofernes.

Chapter Nine

Two Brains Are Better Than One

The professor's study matched his appearance perfectly. Just as hair sprouted at odd angles from his cranium, eyebrows, ears and nostrils, so books, letters and other papers stuck out from every shelf, desk and table. Presumably under the piles of chaos other furniture, like chairs, existed, but the mountains of documents gave no clues as to where.

In other details too there were parallels between the room and its owner. The dingy brown of the decor toned with the fustiness of the Professor's blurred tweed suit. The general untidiness was reflected in the tufts of beard he had missed when shaving. Smoke from an ill-ventilated grate permeated the room, as did fumes from his clenched tobacco pipe. The metal rims of his large spectacles seemed to be echoed in the leading on the window glass.

It was hard to believe that within this scene of chaos ticked one of the finest academic brains of his generation, whose extensive correspondence with experts around the world ensured that his memory was stocked with more information than any encyclopedia. Though never straying outside the walls of St Raphael's, he knew everything there was to know about everything.

Professor Erasmus Holofernes was ecstatic to see Twinks. Whatever his normal reservations about mixing with human-kind during daylight hours, for her he made an exception. 'My dear girl,' he cried in his slightly cracked, over-excited voice, 'this is the best thing that's happened since the invention of cheese. You're looking, as ever, absolutely enchanting.'

With one huge gesture, he swept a precarious pile of books and letters to the floor, revealing underneath them the outline of a leather armchair. 'Please, Twinks, please, take a seat. Now can I offer you something to drink?'

Sitting neatly down and noting the level of squalor preva-lent in the room, Twinks refused his offer. 'Thank you, I just had some coffee,' she lied.

'Coffee?' he echoed as if unfamiliar with the word. Then his brow cleared. 'Yes, of course, I've just poured one for myself,' said the Professor. A doubt struck him. 'Or was that yesterday? Or last week?' He looked vaguely around the room, under whose strata there no doubt lurked many a congealed cup of coffee.

'Don't worry, Razzy,' said Twinks. 'I've come to see you on a criminal matter.'

A light sparkled behind his metal-rimmed glasses. 'It wouldn't be a murder, by any chance, would it?'

'Good ticket. You've winged a partridge with your first shot.'

The Professor rubbed his hands together gleefully. 'This is the best news since the death of Oliver Cromwell. You know how much I love a good succulent murder.'

'Are Scotland Yard consulting you as much as ever?' asked Twinks.

'Oh yes.' He shrugged off the thought. 'But I find them all very simplistic in their reasoning. Shallow minds they have, like all professional policemen. I don't get the intellectual engagement with them that I used to when I was working with you, Twinks.'

She smiled, acknowledging the compliment. There was no point in false modesty. She knew she was possessed of one of the finest deductive brains in the entire world. Matched perhaps only by the brain of the man she was sitting with. They had first met when Scotland Yard, knowing the pair's reputations and baffled by the disappearance of a minor royal's illegitimate son, had brought them together to work on the case. Twinks's understanding of the aristocracy, combined with Professor Holofernes' knowledge of contemporary history, had brought them quickly to a solution which involved two tiger cubs, a cross-dressing bishop and a thieves' kitchen in the vaults beneath St Paul's.

From that time onwards there had been many more pleas for help from Scotland Yard, but generally speaking Holofernes had dealt with them on his own. Though he would have liked to work more with Twinks—even as unworldly a creature as the Professor would have liked to have spent time in her company— she preferred to conduct investigations with her brother. She knew that the ideal aspired to in the world of amateur sleuthdom demanded a wide discrepancy between the intellectual capacity of investigator and sidekick. Twinks and Holofernes were too similar in their gifts, whereas with Blotto at her side she had never had any difficulty in achieving that ideal.

She did, however, retain a great affection for Professor Holofernes and never hesitated to contact him when, as in the current case, she had need of his expertise. So, while he perched on what under its layer of papers was probably a desk, she quickly spelled out the circumstances of the Dowager Duchess of Melmont's murder and the unlawful arrest of Corky Froggett. She watched the Professor's excitement mount as the details emerged. He did a lot of grunting and nodding.

At the end of her narrative, he let a silence elapse before saying slowly, 'Red Hand, Red Hand...I suppose that could be "Crimson Hand".'

'Why? Would that tinkle any cowbells with you, Razzy?'

'It might. It might.' Lugubriously he stroked his whiskery chin. 'This could be a bad business, Twinks.'

She didn't prompt him further. She knew the Professor had his own ways of doing things, and that it was folly to try and make him change them. He leapt suddenly from his perch and homed in like a retriever on a haphazard pile of correspondence carpeting the floor beneath the window. Shuffling through the papers at great speed, rather like the same dog kicking up sand, he quickly found the bulging brown manila files he was looking for.

He spread them out on top of the existing paper mountain of his desk. 'Yes, a bad business, a bad business,' he muttered. With difficulty Twinks managed to hold her tongue as the Professor continued, 'I knew the organization was active on the Continent, but I hoped its evil had not yet invaded our shores. I thought the white cliffs of Dover would have been proof against such a perfidious ideology, but it appears that my optimism was misplaced.'

This time Twinks could no more have stopped herself speaking than a flapper could keep off the dance floor. 'What organization are you talking about, Razzy?'

Professor Erasmus Holofernes peered at her through his thick glasses as though he had forgotten that there was anyone else in the room. And when he spoke, it was more as if he was talking to himself than answering her question. 'It started, like so many pernicious new ideas, in the late 1840s. There had been other groups promoting the evil concept of equality for all before that time, but none of them had caused any major disruption.'

'Erm, Razzy old fruitcake,' Twinks interposed, 'wouldn't you call the French Revolution a major disruption?'

'Oh, that doesn't count.'

'Why not?'

'Because the people behind it were *French*, of course.' Which seemed to end the argument as far as the Professor was concerned. 'Anyway, everything was all right until the 1840s. There were a few isolated stenchers around with misguided notions about everyone being equal, but of course they were all from the oikish classes—you'd never catch a genuine aristocrat having any interest in that kind of guff, would you? And because the bad tomatoes who had those egalitarian ideas were all peasants who couldn't afford to travel anywhere, they were unlikely to meet any others of their persuasion and so couldn't get themselves organized into any kind of protest group.'

'Grandissimo,' murmured Twinks.

'Couldn't agree more. But, like most good things, that state of affairs couldn't continue for ever. In Spain a small number of agricultural workers with ideas above their station formed an organization whose stated aim was to eliminate the aristocracy.'

'"Eliminate"?'

'Kill the lot of them.' Twinks was silent with shock as the appalling implications of this sank in, so the Professor went on: 'These of course were dangerous ideas, spread by people with no understanding of history. From time immemorial in almost all societies the upper classes have owned more or less everything and the rest of the population have slaved away for them— usually for nothing. That's the way things always have worked and the way things always should work. Start messing with that system and chaos ensues. But chaos of course was what said group of Spanish workers was trying to achieve. And...' He paused for effect. '...and this is the important detail, Twinks. That group of workers in Spain was called La Sociedad della Mano Crimisí.'

Since Spanish was one of the thirty-seven languages which Twinks spoke fluently, she had no problem in making the translation. 'So what happened to them, Razzy?' she asked.

'Oh, the proper thing. The ringleaders were rounded up and shot, and their families were turned out of their tied accommodation. Sadly, though eradicating the members of that particular group was easy enough, eradicating their poisonous ideas proved to be a tougher rusk to chew. Further cells developed in Spain, and the contagion spread into France, Italy, Germany...throughout Continental Europe, in fact. There was Der Bund der Blutrote Hand for the Huns, La Société de la Main Cramoisie in France, and so on. And all of them bound by the same vile code. Over the last few decades almost all apparently unexplained murders of European aristocrats can be laid at the door of the League of the Crimson Hand.'

'But did they leave the same deadly imprimatur on the corpses as was found on the Dowager Duchess?'

'My information is that in most cases they did, yes.'

'Then why didn't someone make a connection between the crimes?'

'Twinks...' He let out a pitying sigh. 'Remember we are talking about investigations by Continental police forces. They are even less efficient than our own. Few of them, I imagine, would be able to tell the difference between blood and red paint.'

'True.' Twinks was thoughtful for a moment. 'So the League of the Crimson Hand has been murdering aristocrats on the Continent for some time?'

'Yes.' The Professor shook his head ponderously. 'And now they've somehow infiltrated their way into England.'

A shudder ran through Twinks's slender body. 'I always think it's peculiarly horrid when ghastlinesses like that appear over here. They should stay in Europe, where they belong.'

'Of course,' the Professor reminded her gently, 'England is part of Europe.'

'Only geographically,' snapped Twinks. 'Not in any other way.'

'True. Well, that's what we're up against. A secret society whose vile code encourages them to kill as many of the aristocracy as possible. They have also proved very successful at killing anyone who tries to investigate or infiltrate their organization.'

'Huh.' Twinks looked at her most magnificent as she announced, 'They may have been successful so far, but they haven't yet been challenged by me and Blotto.'

'No.' A sadness spread over Professor Erasmus Holofernes' craggy face. 'I cannot exaggerate the danger of tackling the League of the Crimson Hand. They are conscienceless killers, indifferent to who their victims are. I would strongly discourage anyone from taking them on.' He sighed. 'Though I'm sure my warnings are a waste of breath so far as you are concerned.'

'You're bong on the nose there, Razzy. This is going to be pure creamy éclair for Blotto and me. We'll nab the stenchers and see they're handed over to the proper authorities.'

'May be easier said than done, Twinks. The League of the Crimson Hand are very good at covering their tracks. Will Tyler's going to be as hard to find as one particular piece of plankton in the Pacific Ocean. You don't have any ideas as to where he went, do you?'

'We know he left Snitterings driving an old Napier shooting brake.'

'Probably the one that was found yesterday pushed into the Thames at Shoreditch.'

It never occurred to Twinks to ask where the Professor got this information from. She had long accepted that he did know everything.

'Well, that might mean Will Tyler's still in London.'

'It might. Equally it might not. He would almost definitely have handed the shooting brake over to another League member. Will Tyler could be out of the country by now. You don't have any other leads, do you?'

'As a matter of fact I do.' Twinks reached into her reticule to produce the scrap of paper and the other trophy that she had found in Will Tyler's quarters.

She held up the latter for inspection. 'I don't think there's any doubt what it is,' she announced.

'None at all.' Professor Erasmus Holofernes took it from her and turned it over in his hands. 'An opium pipe. Of Chinese manufacture.' He sniffed the ceramic bowl. 'Last smoked at ten seventeen on Saturday morning.'

'Probably that stencher Tyler bolstering his confidence for the murder of the Dowager Duchess of Melmont.'

'That would be a viable explanation, yes.' The Professor scratched at one of the tufts on his chin. 'So if the murderer has a taste for opium, that might give us a lead to tracking him down.'

'In one of the many opium dens in London?' Twinks suggested excitedly.

'Yes. But which one? There are more of those ghastly places in London these days than there are post-boxes. It could take weeks to check them all out.'

'I wonder if this might be a clue.' Twinks passed across the scrap of paper. 'Found in Will Tyler's spare uniform.'

Professor Erasmus Holofernes scrutinized the evidence. 'Well, at least it gives us another definite link to the League of the Crimson Hand. Pity it's torn.'

'But we do have part of the words that were written on it.'

Both of them looked hard at the enigmatic fragment:

HAI
LEE'S.

'Hmm...I wonder...' And once again the Professor was scurrying round the room, sending papers flying like leaves in an autumn wind. 'Fortunately,' he said, 'I have recently updated my definitive guide to the opium dens of London.' Gleefully he lifted up a battered ring-file and started to flick through its contents.

'Ah, yes!' he cried in triumph. He offered the file to Twinks, one of his ink-stained fingers pressed down on a particular entry.

' "Shanghai Billee's",' she read.

'Exactly! I'll wager my entire brain to a walnut that the missing half of this note contained the letters "SHANG" and "BIL".'

'Yes, of course!' Twinks rose to her feet and replaced the clues in her reticule. 'I can't thank you enough, Razzy!' She bent across to plant a kiss on his unaccustomed cheek. 'I must go!'

Though he knew the answer, Professor Erasmus Holofernes still asked, 'Where to?'

In a cheery shout that shattered the academic calm of St Raphael's, Twinks cried out, 'To Shanghai Billee's!'

Chapter Ten

To London!

'It all sounds a bit of a candle-snuffer,' said Blotto, after his sister had shared with him the fruits of her researches in Oxford. 'You wouldn't have thought anyone—even in the servant classes—would be capable of such stenching behaviour.'

'No, it's all very murdy,' Twinks agreed. 'A wagonload of bad tomatoes, this League of the Crimson Hand.'

'I mean, coffinating people just because of the class they happen to be born into—that's not cricket, is it?'

'Certainly not.'

It was evening at Snitterings. Though Blotto's Lagonda was now safely in one of the garages, they'd decided there was no point in leaving for London till the morning. It was a longish drive and by the time they got there it would be too late to do anything useful. Besides, they needed to put in a bit of planning before they made their assault on Shanghai Billee's.

Blotto still couldn't get over the perniciousness of the League of the Crimson Hand's intentions. 'It's not as if people can help being born into the upper classes. We don't complain about our lot, do we? We just get on with things. You'd have thought people who happen to have been born into the oikish classes would have the decency to do the same.'

'I'm afraid they don't know when they're well off,' said Twinks. 'They seem to have no concept of gratitude.'

'I agree. Well, there's no way the stenchers are going to get away with it. I mean, if they actually succeeded in their plans, it'd be like…it'd be like…' But such was the enormity of the concept that Blotto couldn't find words to express it.

As usual, his sister helped him out. 'It'd make the French Revolution look like a vicarage tea party.'

'Yes.' Blotto pondered the dreadful image for a moment before saying, 'Thank strawberries we found out about it. Because now we'll be able to thwart their evil schemes.'

'Of course we will!' said Twinks, confident as ever.

'Do you think we should tell the Mater what we're planning, me old biscuit barrel?'

'I think we should tell her that we're going to London,' Twinks replied judiciously, 'but I don't think we should tell her why.'

'Good ticket,' said Blotto. Then he hesitated for a moment. 'Will it involve actually lying to the old Madeira cake? Because I never quite feel comfy doing that.'

'Don't worry, me old gumdrop. If there's any lying involved, I'll do it.'

She's a good greengage, my sister, thought Blotto fondly.

'Explain this to me again,' said the Dowager Duchess of Tawcester. 'The two of you suddenly need to go to London tomorrow morning. Could you tell me your reasons?'

'I've just realized that I don't have a stitch to wear for all the round of Christmas parties coming up,' Twinks lied blithely. 'So I'm going to see my couturier in Bond Street.'

'That sounds perfectly acceptable.' Then the Dowager Duchess turned her dinosauric eye on her younger son. 'And what about you, Blotto? I cannot imagine that you wish to attend your sister's sartorial discussions.'

'No, Mater.'

'So why are you accompanying her? Is it a visit to your tailor in Savile Row?'

'No, Mater.'

'Your shirt-maker in Jermyn Street?'

'No, Mater.'

'Your gun-maker in St James's?'

'No, Mater.'

'Then why are you going to London?'

Blotto squirmed. He looked to his sister for help. Twinks, rather enjoying his discomfiture, smiled mischievously.

'Blotto,' his mother thundered, 'you are not going the way of the Duchess of Herrington's boy, are you?'

'I don't know which way the Duchess of Herrington's boy went, Mater.'

'He has been a severe disappointment to her—and to the rest of his family. He has let down his entire heritage by developing something which I believe he refers to as a "social conscience". He has taken recently to going to London and distributing soup to the poor. I would, needless to say, be profoundly vexed were I to discover that any child of mine had ventured on such a course.' The unblinking eyes were once again focused on her wretched son. 'Blotto, you are not going to London to do good works, are you?'

With complete honesty, he was able to reassure her that this was not the purpose of his visit.

'Thank goodness for that. If you had taken such a course, I would never be able to hold my head up amongst my equals again.'

Blotto looked relieved at being off the hook. But his stay of execution was of course only temporary. 'So why are you going to London?' the Dowager Duchess asked implacably.

Her son's mouth made the desperate movements of a goldfish trying to remember what the other side of its bowl looked like. 'Erm…erm…erm…' he stuttered.

Finally Twinks took pity on him. 'What Blotto is going to do, Mater, is go to his club and join up with a lot of other boddos and slurp down the champers until he gets entirely wobbulated.'

A rare smile of nostalgia spread across the Dowager Duchess's craggy features. 'Just exactly as his father used to do.' She turned the deadly beam on to her son. 'That, of course, is perfectly in order, Blotto.'

He always got a fizzulating charge out of being on the open road in the Lagonda. It was a crisp autumn morning, one of those peculiar English ones which were summer in the sun and winter in the shade. But he and his sister were happy to brave the elements with the Lagonda's roof down. Both wore goggles and leather helmets, and even in such unflattering headgear Twinks looked marvellous. Their leather suitcases were strapped on to the rack over the dickey at the back, and both of their minds were effervescing with the thought of a new adventure.

For Blotto there was another cause of joy. Every mile the Lagonda put between him and Snitterings was a mile further away from the unwanted attentions of Laetitia Melmont.

That morning he didn't even mind that their destination was London, a city whose close-packed buildings usually cast a shadow over his wide-open-space-loving spirits. Going there was a necessary step in the eradication of the threat presented by the League of the Crimson Hand. And he'd seen his beloved Tawcester Towers only the day before when he'd gone to pick up the Lag.

As they had done when they were children, Blotto and Twinks whiled away the journey by playing I-Spy. As it had done when they were children, the game proved to be a rather frustrating experience for Twinks. While she chose objects inside the car for her brother to guess, Blotto always chose things outside the vehicle, which frequently, by the time he gave their initial letter to his sister, turned out to be miles behind them.

Very rarely was he able to best her in any intellectual exercise. Very rarely in the nursery had he been able to thumb his nose to her and utter the cry of childhood triumph: 'So snubbins to you, Twinks!'

Their mood sobered as the Lagonda slowed and they started to grind through North London's thickening traffic and greater density of buildings. Blotto and Twinks both felt increasingly aware of the seriousness of their mission. As the villas of leafy suburbs gave way to smaller, grimy, gardenless dwellings, neither of them could remove from their minds that, amongst the oikish people who lived in them, there might be some who subscribed to the appalling precepts of the League of the Crimson Hand.

In a sooty inner suburb Blotto had to stop at a filling station to top up the Lagonda's tank with petroleum. And while, under his watchful eye, a grubby artisan manned the pump, he was suddenly aware of a strange sound which seemed to be emanating from the car's dickey. Intrigued, Blotto moved closer.

Yes, there definitely was something. A tapping, scraping noise and a mewing.

Blotto was puzzled. The dickey was a folding contraption, whose seat and back pressed close together when it was closed. There was no room there for a human being to squash in. But he supposed it was possible that one of the Snitterings cats had crept in when the dickey was open and found itself an unwilling prisoner when the door was slammed shut.

He gestured to Twinks to come round from the passenger seat and make her own judgement of the phenomenon. 'Must be a cat,' he suggested.

His sister was unconvinced. 'It sounds to me like a human making that noise.'

'But a human wouldn't fit in there.'

Uncharacteristically serious, Twinks looked her brother in the eye. 'Removing the seat and back would allow someone to get in. I wouldn't have thought that was beyond the wit of a member of the League of the Crimson Hand.'

Blotto gasped. Deftly he opened his leather suitcase on its rack, and drew out his trusty cricket bat. He held it poised over the door of the dickey and gestured to Twinks.

She flicked the handle open and jumped back to avoid potential gunfire.

The leather seat components had indeed been removed, and the dickey did contain a human being. But it wasn't anyone from the League of the Crimson Hand. It was Laetitia Melmont.

She looked up coyly at Blotto. 'You rescued me! My hero!'

Chapter Eleven

Shanghai Billee's

Being so close to their destination, Blotto and Twinks could not even consider turning round and delivering the stowaway back to Snitterings. Twinks wanted to drop her at a railway terminus so that she could return by train, but Laetitia claimed to be terrified by the idea. She had never in her life travelled on public transport and she could not tolerate the close proximity of people from the oikish classes. Twinks tried to explain to her the system of First, Second and Third Class compartments, which had been expressly designed for the admirable purpose of separating those who could afford more from those who couldn't, but her words fell on deaf ears.

And then Blotto, who Twinks would have expected to have wanted rid of their supernumerary passenger even more than she did, turned chivalrous. He announced that they couldn't possibly allow the poor girl to be alone in a city where she had never before travelled without a huge retinue of servants. It was their duty never to let Laetitia out of their sight.

Twinks was forced yet again to observe that her brother was a fool to himself. He was ensuring that they would be stuck with 'the Snitterings Ironing-Board', and, what was more, his actions on her behalf would be construed as further proof of the love Laetitia was still convinced he felt for her. Which would play into the hands of the Dowager Duchess and her match-making plans. Chivalry could sometimes be awful guff, thought Twinks.

London grew dingier and dingier as the Lagonda nosed its way into the East End. Visibility shrank as the autumn gloom was augmented by fog. If an ordinary fog in the city was known as a 'London Peculiar', then that day's was very peculiar indeed. If it was known as a 'peasouper', then that day the soup had been made with insufficient stock and the peas hadn't been properly puréed.

There were few other cars around on the dark streets. Dilapidated wagons were pulled along by spavined drayhorses, frightened-looking men dragged handcarts. Though it was only late afternoon, in the narrow space between looming buildings the autumn sun had not penetrated down as far as the roadway. The high-bred noses of the party in the Lagonda were assailed by smells of river mud, rotting fish and other less mentionable aromas. Even the ebullient spirits of Blotto and Twinks were cast down by the squalor that surrounded them. And Laetitia Melmont, hitherto unaware that human beings could survive in such conditions, looked about her, open-mouthed with disbelief.

In the dark, fogbound streets the Lagonda gleamed like a pearl in a rotten oyster.

Twinks, who was good at navigation as well as everything else, gave Blotto directions from a map which Professor Erasmus Holofernes had drawn for her. Neither of them could suppress a feeling of dread as they approached their destination.

Without the map they would never have found Shanghai Billee's, so filthy and insignificant was its entrance. Glimpses of scummy water through gaps between nearby buildings, as well as the more intense stench of fetid mud, suggested they were very close to the Thames, and indeed that the opium den must be right on the waterfront.

When the Lagonda drew to a halt outside the filthy doorway, over which hung an even filthier scrap of canvas, brother and sister exchanged looks. Twinks's head almost imperceptibly jerked towards Laetitia Melmont in the dickey, and the expression in her azure eyes demanded: What are we going to do about her?

But Blotto had already decided. Turning towards their unwelcome passenger, he announced, 'Laetitia, I'm going to put the roof up. You sit inside the car and I'll lock it. Whatever you do, don't open the door to anyone until we come back. Tickey-tockey?'

'Absolutely tickey-tockey,' she replied, then, simpering, said once again, 'I do so love it when you're masterful, Blotto.'

He realized that he was getting deeper and deeper into the gluepot so far as Laetitia Melmont was concerned, and at some point the problem of extricating himself from her talons would have to be faced. But time enough for a solution there. At that moment he had more urgent priorities.

Silently he put up the Lagonda's roof, ushered Laetitia into the passenger seat and, pausing only to pick up his cricket bat, locked the car doors. Then, turning to his sister with an expression of impossibly brave determination, asked, 'Loins girded, Twinks me old fruitbat?'

'Loins girded, Blotto me old bloater.'

'Ready to meet Dr Fu Manchu, are you?'

'Erm...Dr Fu Manchu doesn't exist, Blotto. He's just a character in books.'

Any other time he would have stopped to take issue with his sister on this point. In a life of minimal reading, the works of Sax Rohmer were amongst the very few that Blotto had ever enjoyed. He fully believed in the evil Doctor's ambition of world domination and he knew how important it was that the man was stopped before his evil tentacles had...

But Blotto recognized that this was not the moment to put Twinks right on the reality of Fu Manchu. Time enough for that. Instead, with a boyishly bold grin to his sister, he called out, 'Right, in we go!'

And Blotto pushed aside the frayed and filthy canvas that hung over the entrance to Shanghai Billee's.

In the interior there was so little light—its sources only a couple of guttering candles and a glowing brazier—that it took a moment or two for their eyes to accommodate. They could hardly breathe in the fog of opium fumes that assaulted their nostrils. When they could see, they were greeted by a scene of terrible human degradation.

On makeshift straw-filled mattresses around the room lay the flotsam and jetsam of ruined lives. Thin light from the candles flickered across pale parchment-like faces of men who had escaped their miseries for a little while in the oblivion of the pernicious drug. Here and there embers glowed in the bowls of pipes from which their owners sucked a lingering death. Twinks immediately visualized that another circle of hell had been added to Dante's Inferno. Blotto, who wasn't such a whale on literary allusion (except, of course, for Fu Manchu), reckoned the place was a spoffing great stench-hole.

An emaciated figure in a faded blue robe shuffled towards them. On his head was a grubby skullcap and a greasy black pigtail hung down his back. His thin yellow face was as inscrutable as a carving in an oriental temple.

'You comee wrong placee,' he said. 'This no placee for ladee.'

'No,' said Twinks boldly, 'we've come to the right place. Are you Shanghai Billee?'

'Billee no here,' the man replied. 'You goee. You comee wrong placee.'

'Do you have to talk like that?' asked Blotto.

'Whatee you meanee?'

'Adding "ee" to the end of every word. I don't think it's really necessary.'

'Oh.' The man looked nonplussed, then went on, 'Mostee people likee talkee likee this. Essential partee of opium denee experience.'

'Well, we'd rather you spoke proper English,' said Blotto.

'Oh, very well.' The Chinaman looked rather disgruntled at having his routine taken away, but grudgingly continued in a voice with a cockney twang. 'Anyway, you two shouldn't be in here. It's no place for people of your class.'

'Don't come that class card guff with us,' said Twinks. 'We're here because we're investigating a murder.'

'Oh yes?' A new caution came into the man's thin eyes. 'There've been no murders here at Shanghai Billee's. Some customers may have succumbed to the effects of the drug and died, but no one has been deliberately murdered. Maybe you've come to the wrong opium den. Perhaps you should try Singapore Fred's—they've had lots of murders there.'

'We aren't talking about a murder happening in here,' explained Blotto. 'We just think you might be harbouring a murderer.'

'And there he is.' Twinks, who had been peering into the dark corners of the room, pointed a finger to one of the noisome mattresses on which lay a lanky figure whose features proclaimed him to be of British stock. Though his face was now pale and woozy from opium, she had had no difficulty in comparing him with the stored image from Proops's staff photograph. It was Will Tyler.

'I don't know whether he's a murderer or not,' said the Chinaman. 'Not my business. So long as they pay, we don't ask anyone no questions in here.'

'Tickey-tockey for you,' said Twinks. 'We on the other hand are going to ask the stencher some questions.'

The thin shoulders shrugged. 'You can do what you want, but one thing I should tell you. Nobody does anything in Shanghai Billee's for nothing.'

'Maybe this will help.' Blotto removed a crisp white fiver from his blazer and proffered it to the man. In a movement so swift as almost to be imperceptible, the note was tucked away inside the greasy robe.

'You'll get a lot of opium for that. Do you both want pipes?'

Twinks was about to refuse with some vigour, but she was silenced by a gesture from her brother. 'Yes, thank you,' he said. And while the Chinaman busied himself by the brazier preparing the pipes, Blotto murmured, 'Thought it'd be a good wheeze, Twinks. If we have pipes we won't look out of place in here.'

She contemplated telling him that very few of the other people in the den were wearing blazers and cricket flannels—or indeed rose silk travelling costumes and mink coats—but she restrained herself. Blotto was always so boyishly proud of his ideas that she never liked to pancake them.

The Chinaman handed across two scorched and filthy pipes, in whose bowls lumps of burning opium glowed, then seemed to lose interest in his visitors and disappeared into the recesses of the den.

'Probably be a good ticket not to inhale this murdy stuff,' whispered Blotto.

'I had thought of that,' his sister replied. But the way she held the pipe-stem in her teeth looked very professional. Twinks did quite often smoke cigarettes, and Blotto was very proud of her for that. She was so dashed modern.

No one in the opium den took the slightest notice of them as they moved closer to the stinking mattress on which Will Tyler lay. Some of the clientele were insensible, and those who weren't were interested only in finding insensibility.

Twinks and Blotto, still holding his trusty cricket bat, sat on the insalubrious floor beside Tyler. Through the cracks between its rotting planks they could see light catch on the greasy water. The building was actually built on piles projecting over the Thames.

The Snitterings footman seemed to be in a state between sleep and waking. When Twinks spoke his name, his eyelids flickered, but the effort of opening them defeated him.

'Look, you stencher, about you murdering the Dowager Duchess of Melmont...' Blotto began, but a slight shake of the head from his sister stopped him.

'I think we need to be a bit subtler,' she whispered.

'Tickey-tockey,' he whispered back, knowing that when it came to subtlety, Twinks was the lark's larynx and he was a dead dormouse.

'Tyler,' said Twinks, her voice suddenly taking on the tone that she used when she addressed dogs or horses, and which her mother used when addressing anyone, 'you have done well. I am sent, on behalf of the League of the Crimson Hand, to congratulate you. The murder at Snitterings was beautifully executed.'

'I was only doing my duty,' the drugged footman mumbled.

'And you discharged that duty admirably. Do you know what your next duty will be?'

'I am awaiting instructions. Anything the League of the Crimson Hand demands of me, I will perform.' He spoke these words more like an automaton than a human being. Twinks wondered what devilish methods had been used to subjugate his will to that of the evil organization of which he was a mere puppet. He was now in the vile bondage of opium, but she feared that before that his brain might have been polluted by other hallucinators from the criminal pharmacopoeia.

'Your next duty,' the deep-voiced Twinks continued, 'will take you to the headquarters of the League of the Crimson Hand.'

'I do not know where the headquarters of the League of the Crimson Hand are. None of we operatives knows its precise location, for reasons of security.'

'You will be informed of how to get there,' said Twinks, following up some details of the organization's workings that had been given her by Professor Erasmus Holofernes. 'You will receive that information from your contact in the cell above you.'

'From Davy ap Dafydd?' asked Will Tyler blearily.

'Yes, from Davy ap Dafydd.' Twinks salted away the name for future reference. 'He is still your contact?'

'Yes. He is the next Letter-Bearer.'

'Letter-Bearer?' Twinks echoed, hoping that in his drugged state the footman would not find her ignorance odd.

Fortunately he showed no suspicion as he responded, 'I am the Letter-Bearer of the Little Finger.'

Blotto looked blankly at his sister. He hoped she was making more sense of Will Tyler's replies than he was. As usual, that wouldn't be difficult.

'Show me the Little Finger,' Twinks commanded.

Still acting more like a machine than a man, Will Tyler raised his grubby right hand towards her. Firmly she took hold and moved it closer to the guttering candlelight. She licked one of her own fingers and wiped off the grime on the pad of his smallest digit.

Tattooed on the flesh in crimson ink were the four letters: 'GGEC'.

'What does it mean?' asked Twinks urgently. 'What do the letters mean?'

'They are my link to Davy ap Dafydd,' the footman replied, his voice dull and listless.

'And does he too have letters tattooed on his little finger?' Twinks demanded, excitement bubbling within her.

Tyler shook his befuddled head. 'No. I am the only Letter-Bearer of the Little Finger.'

As ever, she caught on quickly. 'You mean that Davy ap Dafydd is the Letter-Bearer of the Ring Finger?' Her conjecture was rewarded by a nod. 'Then there will be Letter-Bearers for the Middle Finger, the Index Finger and the Thumb?'

'There is no Letter-Bearer for the Thumb. The Crimson Thumb is our master, the one who controls everyone else.'

'And do you know who he is?' asked Twinks, more in hope than in expectation of getting the answer.

Her judgement had been correct. Will Tyler replied, 'No one knows the identity of the Crimson. Thumb.'

'But when we have found all four Letter-Bearers, we will know the way into League of the Crimson Hand's headquarters, the place from which the Crimson Thumb operates?'

Blotto watched amazed, as another nod confirmed that his sister was on the right track. How did she do it? How many normal-sized spoffing brains would it take to provide the horse-power that fitted into Twinks's delicate cranium?

She pressed home her advantage. 'And, Tyler, do you know any of the other Letter-Bearers? Except for Davy ap Dafydd, the one in the cell above yours?'

His reply sounded like something that had been learned by rote, probably dinned into his memory while he was under the influence of another noxious mind-changing potion. 'I only know one other name. The name of the person in the cell above mine. It is Davy ap Dafydd. In this way are kept secret all activities of the League of the Crimson Hand. I take orders directly from only one other member of the League. That is Davy ap Dafydd.'

'Who do you give orders to? What is the name of the person in the cell below you?' demanded Twinks.

But her hopes for another lead were quickly dashed. 'There is no cell below mine,' Will Tyler replied. 'I am just a foot soldier, right at the bottom of the heap.'

'And you don't know the name of anyone in any cell above yours, except for Davy ap Dafydd?'

The weary head shook slowly. His eyelids were near to giving up their unequal struggle against closure.

'Tell me one more thing,' Twinks urged. 'How do you make contact with Davy ap Dafydd when you need to?'

The footman's eyes swam as he tried to focus on his inter-rogator. 'We are sworn not to reveal that information on pain of death.'

Relying on his befuddlement to cloud his judgement, Twinks responded: 'Not to reveal that information to anyone outside the League of the Crimson Hand, of course. But you know I am a senior officer of the League. I answer only to the Crimson Thumb himself.'

Drugged he may have been, but he wasn't so disoriented as to take her assertion at face value. 'How do I know that?' he asked.

'Because,' Twinks thundered, sounding more than ever like her mother, 'I came here to express the League's gratitude for the good job you did on our behalf at Snitterings.'

It worked. 'Oh yes, of course you did. So what is it you want from me now?'

'How is it that you make contact with Davy ap Dafydd?'

'It is always done the same way. I place an encoded small advertisement in the Personal Column of the *Daily Clarion*. Davy ap Dafydd replies with another advertisement, which tells the time and place of our next meeting.'

'So you always meet in a different place?'

'Well, we're meant to, but we don't,' the footman admitted with confused sheepishness. 'Fact is, there's a pub we both like and it's convenient, so we always meet there.' Suddenly he looked alarmed. 'But I shouldn't have told you that, should I, what with you being a high-up from the League of the Crimson Hand?'

'I will not pass on news of your lapse in security precautions...' said Twinks solemnly, 'so long as you tell me the name and location of the pub where you and Davy ap Dafydd are in the habit of meeting.'

'But I—'

'Tell me!' Twinks used the voice that had claimed the walls of Jerusalem during the Crusades, the voice that had rallied the English bowmen at Agincourt, the voice that had ordered floggings on many ships of the Royal Fleet, the voice that assumed there was nobody else in any restaurant. Someone of Will Tyler's background could no more have resisted the command of that voice than he could have pronounced an 'aitch' properly.

'The pub is a real hell-hole. Davy ap Dafydd likes it, though, because it's called The Three—'

But Blotto and Twinks didn't find out The Three What. A gunshot sounded, disproportionately loud in the cramped space.

And a bloody hole appeared in the centre of Will Tyler's forehead. With an expression of increased befuddlement, he sank back on to his filthy mattress. Dead.

Chapter Twelve

Conflagration!

Blotto turned immediately to where the shot had come from and was rewarded by the sight of a pigtailed figure in a loose smock, black trousers and conical hat zapping out of the den like a cheetah on spikes. With a cry of, 'Bring down the portcullis, Twinks me old pineapple, and I'll catch the stencher!' he rushed off in hot pursuit. An emaciated figure rose from the floor to block his way, but a neat reverse sweep from Blotto's cricket bat sent the man flying. His flailing arms hit the brazier, which fell sideways, scattering hot coals over the wooden floor.

Blotto was already out in the foggy street before that happened. The Chinese gunman had a good start on him, but constant hunting and fielding practice kept Blotto in tickey-tockey trim. In only a few strides he had overhauled the assassin and downed him with a rugby tackle bang from the jolly old textbook (which is not an easy action to perform for a man carrying a cricket bat).

The man wriggled in his grasp like an oiled eel, and managed to free the hand which still held his gun, an Accrington-Murphy .44 revolver. Just in time Blotto was aware of the barrel being moved round towards his face. Quarters were too close for him to use the cricket bat, so he grabbed at the Chinaman's wrist to force the gun away. He seemed to be succeeding, but then heard a gunshot and felt the passage of a bullet through his blond thatch. The sound had come from behind him, back at the entrance to Shanghai Billee's. Out of this now poured seven or eight men who had, only moments before, been apparently comatose on the floor. Through the fog it could be seen that most of them were carrying guns, and those without had knives and axes.

Still clasped to the killer of Will Tyler, Blotto rolled over, so that his opponent's body was now between him and the new attackers. But he knew that using the assassin as a human shield would only afford him temporary protection. Anyway, it wasn't the way he liked to fight. Englishmen of his class didn't hide behind things. They stood up to face any music—or in this case, gunfire—that was coming their way.

So that's what he did. Pausing only to immobilize his opponent with a good whack on the head from his bat and to tie the man by his pigtail to a convenient lamp-post, Blotto rose to face his aggressors. As he strode forward into the murk, he waited for the men he approached to become aware of that indefinable superiority which is given to the British upper classes, and to shrink backwards from his presence.

Sadly, such displays of deference did not seem to have formed part of the education of this particular bunch of bad tomatoes. Shouting curses in a language unfamiliar to Blotto, the pigtailed posse advanced towards him in a cautious semi-circle. Fire spat from one of their guns. A bullet nipped the nap of his blazer. A second gunshot flicked the fuzz off his flannels. Though the Chinamen were clearly rotten shots, the law of averages—if nothing else—dictated that a bullet was going to hit him before too long. Blotto had to take action.

Fixing the firm, two-handed grip on the handle of his bat that he'd been taught at Eton by 'Pinko' Fripworth, he moved in sudden zigzags towards his opponents. He heard the whine of bullets like hornets about his head, the scream of those which kicked up from the cobbles beneath his feet, as he thrust into the midst of his enemies and proceeded to give the vile anarchists a lesson in the strokes of cricket.

Dropping almost to one knee, with a Paddle Sweep to the shins, he felled two Chinamen, whose collapse brought down a third. A steady Block countered a descending axe, which was driven into the face of its bearer. A pistol was sent flying from a trigger-squeezing hand by a fine Hook Shot, whose follow-through caught another assailant plum on the point of his chin.

The fight seemed to have gone out of the two remaining assailants, who turned and fled, the last one receiving a perfectly executed Slog across his buttocks from the doughty bat of Blotto.

As he stood with his back to Shanghai Billee's, surveying the scene of his triumph, Blotto became aware of unseasonal warmth behind him. Also the crackling sound of ravenous flames.

He turned in horror to see the conflagration which had once been an opium den. Despite the damp from the river, the scattered coals of the overturned brazier must quickly have fired the rotten flooring. Shanghai Billee's had turned instantly from one kind of hell-hole to another. Twinks's mental image of Dante's Inferno was now being made real.

Blotto of course knew nothing of his sister's literary allusions. All he knew was that he couldn't see Twinks. Shouting her name, he hurled himself back into the flaming opium den.

But before he was through the doorway, the whole structure exploded as if the flames had reached some hidden stash of gunpowder. Blotto was hurled back by the force of the blast to the other side of the road, where he crashed through the dusty glass frontage of an empty ship-chandlery.

By the time Blotto had picked himself up and removed splinters of wood and glass from his hair and clothing, Shanghai Billee's was no more. Through the smoky space where it had stood, now like a missing tooth between the adjacent hovels, he could see the filthy, churning waters of the Thames.

Of his beautiful sister there was no sign.

'Twinks!' he cried out. 'Twinks! Where are you?'

Chapter Thirteen

Salvation!

The Honourable Devereux Lyminster was not given to introspection, and his customary outlook on life made Pollyanna look like one of the world's worst doom-mongers. He generally greeted each morning with a twinkle in his eye and a bounce in his step. He didn't know the meaning of the word 'depression' (mind you, there were quite a lot of other words he didn't know the meaning of either).

But at that moment, facing the ruins of Shanghai Billee's, uncertain as to whether his sister's life had been claimed by fire or drowning, his mood was uncharacteristically lugubrious. Oh, broken biscuits, he said to himself. Biscuits broken into very small pieces indeed!

As he turned away from the wreckage, in the vain hope of seeing his sister on dry land, he found himself repeating out loud his earlier question, 'Twinks! Twinks, where are you?'

There was a silence longer than that which would have followed the announcement to his mother that he was going to marry a chorus girl.

Then he heard distantly the perky cry of, 'I'm here, Blotto me old trouser button!'

Turning again towards the ruins of Shanghai Billee's, he could at first see nothing through the mingled smoke and fog, but then he caught a glimpse of a slender arm waving from the waters of the Thames beyond.

He rushed to the water's edge and, standing on a still-burning beam, shouted, 'I'm coming in to get you, me old kipper!'

'Don't be a Grade A poodle!' the reply came back. 'You know I'm a strong enough swimmer to represent Great Britain at the sport, but for the fact that only oikish people do that kind of thing.'

As if to prove her point, Twinks struck out and, with a few short efficient strokes from her sylphlike limbs, was soon alongside her brother. She reached up her arm and with one firm pull Blotto had her out of the water.

Twinks, though drenched to the skin and covered with slime whose provenance it wouldn't have been tasteful to go into, still managed to look stylish. Though her blonde hair was plastered round the outline of her skull, the azure eyes had lost none of their sparkle.

'I'd forgotten what a lark swimming can be,' she trilled. 'Absolute larksissimo. I must do more of it.'

'But you're as wet as a Riviera sponger,' said Blotto, removing his blazer. 'Here, put this round the old shoulder-blades.'

Twinks did as he suggested, and moved closer to the smouldering debris of the opium den. 'Shanghai Billee's can do me the final service of drying me out.'

She looked round at the groggy and groaning Chinamen on the roadway. 'Your doing, I assume, Blotto?'

He grinned in self-deprecation. 'Oh, I did have a bit of help.'

'Who from?'

'Oh, no actual boddos. Just mean it wasn't only my dukes and the Marquis of Queensberry. I used the cricket bat too,' he added apologetically.

'I don't think you need feel bad about that,' said Twinks, who had a reputation as an arbiter in matters of chivalry and derring-do. She looked down at the scattering of discarded firearms on the road. 'Some of the stenchers did have guns, after all.'

'Yes, I suppose so.' But his tone showed he wasn't quite convinced. Defeating bad tomatoes with one's bare hands would always slightly have the edge over using a weapon.

'Anyway,' he went on, remembering the circumstances which had got him into the fight, 'do you have any tinkling what happened to that Will Tyler lump of toadspawn?'

'Well, he was coffinated the minute the bullet binged him. Then the whole rombooley went into the drink. I'd imagine in a couple of days' time the Thames River Police would find something nasty on the end of their boathooks.'

'Do you know if any of the Chinamen got one-way tickets?'

'I should think a few must have done. Nobody could have come out of that inferno alive.'

'You did, Twinks.'

'Yes, but, well…' It was a rare moment of his sister looking sheepish. Though she had no problem with being extolled for her beauty and intellectual capacity, she always felt a bit shy about her physical achievements.

Cheerily Blotto changed the subject. 'Anyway, at least I bagged the important one alive.'

'Sorry?'

'The stencher who coffinated Tyler. I've got him tied up to that lamp-post over there.'

But, as his own eye followed his gesture, Blotto could see that the murderer had got away. All that remained on closer inspection was a pigtail tied to the lamp-post. And it wasn't even a real pigtail. It was a pigtail wig.

'Rodents!' he said, as he showed the object to his sister. 'What does this mean, Twinks?'

'It means that the League of the Crimson Hand's tentacles stretch further than we thought.' Blotto looked characteristically blank. 'And there's more evidence of it.'

He looked where she was pointing, and noticed something strange was happening to the faces of the unconscious Chinamen nearest to the blaze that had once been Shanghai Billee's. The pigmentation which so distinguished them from British citizens was melting and trickling away in the heat, to reveal pink flesh underneath.

'Toad-in-the-hole, Twinks! What's going on?'

'You've heard of the "Yellow Peril", Blotters, haven't you?'

'Of course I have. It's the evil scheme, masterminded by Dr Fu Manchu, for the civilized world to be taken over by the powers of the Orient.'

'Yes, that's what we're meant to think. As a result, we're meant to distrust people of other, faraway nations.'

'Well, doing that's not such a tough rusk to chew, is it? I mean, if you're British, it is a kind of instinct.'

'But it's not true. Our thoughts are being manipulated.'

'Sorry, you're going to have to spell this one out for me, Twinks me old tin tray. Come on, uncage the ferrets.'

'Very well. How useful for people who want to disrupt the government of a country it is to get the people frightened by some external threat.'

'Exactly what I was saying, Twinks. That's where the Yellow Peril and Dr Fu Manchu come in.'

'No, Blotto. That's where we're meant to believe that the Yellow Peril and Dr Fu Manchu come in.' Once again, she had her brother bewildered. 'Look at these men.' She crouched down and rubbed the face of one of Blotto's victims. Her finger came up stained with yellow. 'Greasepaint. As used in pantomimes and music halls. These thugs have not come from China. It's a guinea to a groat that the furthest they've come from is Wapping.'

To prove her point further, she felt along the man's hairline and removed another pigtail wig, revealing the mousy thatch beneath.

There was a silence. Then Blotto said, 'I'm afraid my touchpaper hasn't ignited yet, Twinks.'

'What has happened,' she explained patiently, 'is that the Western World has been the victim of a conspiracy to make us distrust the Eastern World. Disguising thugs like this is part of the process of convincing us that we face the threat of a Yellow Peril, a Yellow Peril that doesn't exist.'

Blotto was flabbergasted. 'Twinks, are you saying that the Yellow Peril doesn't exist?'

'That's just what I did say, Blotto.'

'Yes, but did you mean it?'

'Of course I meant it. The Yellow Peril is a fabrication of evil men who wish to destabilize the good relations between nations.'

'Well, I'll be jugged like a hare!' said Blotto. 'And who are these evil men?'

'The League of the Crimson Hand,' replied Twinks. She shifted Blotto's blazer around her elegant shoulders before announcing, 'And now I think it's time for me to have a very deep, hot bath.'

'What, we're going to Lyminster House, are we?'

Blotto referred to the Tawcesters' London base, a large mansion in Mayfair, which was kept permanently staffed and ready for any family members who might need it.

'No,' said Twinks.

'Why not?'

'Sloggo's staying there.'

She did not need to say any more. Blotto and Twinks tolerated their sister-in-law at Tawcester Towers, because she and the Duke had their own wing of the house and the place was big enough for the four of them not to meet very much. But the thought of Sloggo's company for a whole evening in the cramped conditions of the twelve-bedroomed London house was more than either of them could cope with.

'Good ticket,' said Blotto. 'So what do we do?'

'We book a suite at the Savoy,' his sister replied as she started towards the Lagonda.

'Just one thing, Twinks,' asked Blotto plaintively. 'All that guff you were saying about the Yellow Peril...does it mean that Dr Fu Manchu really doesn't exist?'

When they reached the Lagonda, they found that its fabric roof had been slit open with a knife. And there was no sign of Laetitia Melmont inside.

'Great whiffling water rats!' said Twinks. 'The League of the Crimson Hand have got her!'

Chapter Fourteen

Three What?

Blotto and Twinks had no difficulty in procuring a suite at the Savoy. The Tawcester name still counted for something, and the family of a Huddersfield mining magnate, in London to celebrate his daughter's wedding, were quickly shunted off to inferior accommodation. After brother and sister had soaked off the grime of Limehouse in the separate bathrooms of their suite, they changed into evening dress (intending to dine later in the Grill downstairs) and reconvened in the sitting room over cocktails sent up from the bar.

Generally speaking, cocktails weren't Blotto's cut of the joint. He liked his spirits ungarnished—brandy or whisky with the merest whoosh from the soda syphon. But, as in all things, he bowed to his sister's greater knowledge and sophistication. Twinks kept abreast with all the latest fashions in drinking, and had a network of chums to keep her informed of the latest creations by every barman in London. She had heard that in the cocktail world the new incumbent in the Savoy was a whale amongst whales.

'I'm going to go for the Cobbler's Awl,' she had confided to Blotto after consulting the list of possibilities.

'What's in that?'

'Oh, about seven different spirits, two contrasting champagnes and a dash of absinthe.'

'Sounds beezer. Shall I go for one of the same?'

'Don't think so, Blotto. A Cobbler's Awl is a bit of a ladies' drink.'

'Oh. So what'd fit my pigeon-hole?'

'I think a St Louis Steamhammer would match your sock-suspenders, Blotto.'

'Right, a St Louis Steamhammer it is, Twinks me old muffin.'

As ever, his sister's choice had been impeccable. Deciding sensibly that one cocktail might not be enough to see them through their discussion of the case, when ordering on the internal telephone Twinks had requested that a full shaker of each of their choices should be delivered to the suite. The Room Service waiter was commendably speedy in discharging his duty. He arrived, filled the appropriate glass for each of the guests, and left the two cocktail shakers on ice. He had also, at the request of Twinks, brought up a commercial directory of London phone numbers.

When he had left the room, Twinks toasted their enterprise. 'To tracking down the other men with tattooed fingers!' she said as she raised her glass.

'Good ticket!' said Blotto, raising his.

'And to finding Laetitia Melmont!' Twinks continued.

'Oh yes,' Blotto agreed with a little less enthusiasm. In the warm comfort of his bath he'd managed to forget that little problem. Also to forget the inevitable pressures towards matrimony that would be exerted by his mother when he did rescue 'the Snitterings Ironing-Board'.

'And to the destruction of the League of the Crimson Hand!' Twinks concluded in a ringing voice.

There fortunately was a sentiment with which Blotto had no problem in agreeing. He took a long swallow from his St Louis Steamhammer.

The effect was not immediate. He tasted a sweetness on his tongue, a sweetness with a slight tang of asperity, but nothing else seemed to happen. He grinned amiably at his sister, who had just taken a delicate sip of her Cobbler's Awl and was also waiting to feel the benefit.

Then Blotto understood the reason for the St Louis Steamhammer's name. He felt as though he had been tapped firmly on the head by a blunt instrument upholstered in velvet. Not just one tap, but an accelerating crescendo of taps, building to a drum roll of sensation that reverberated through his skull, bouncing and echoing off the bony interior of his cranium. He wouldn't be surprised to find that small jets of blue steam were being expelled through his ears.

'Toad-in-the-hole...' Blotto murmured. It was his highest form of praise.

'The Cobbler's Awl is larksissimo too,' said Twinks reverently. But then she got down to business. 'Now listen, Blotto me old gumdrop, we've actually achieved the first part of our mission...'

'Have we?' he asked, confused.

'Yes. Our first aim was to track down the murderer of the Dowager Duchess of Melmont, so that we can get Corky Froggett released. That has been achieved. As we thought, Will Tyler was the perpetrator. He admitted as much.'

'Yes. And now he's dead,' said Blotto, a shadow crossing his face. 'Which is a bit of a candle-snuffer, because it means we can't hand him over to the proper authorities.'

'I'm sure Inspector Trumbull and Sergeant Knatchbull will survive the disappointment.'

'Yes, but that's a bit of our investigations that I always enjoy. You know, when we've solved the case—or rather you've solved the case—and you write up all the evidence into a dossier and pass it over to Inspector Trumbull and Sergeant

Knatchbull. And then they always manage to convince themselves that they reached the conclusion under their own steam.'

'Well, I'm afraid we're going to miss out on that bit of the investigation, so far as Will Tyler's concerned.' Then, to blow away the residual gloom on her brother's face, Twinks continued, 'But think how fizzulated the ancient Inspector and Sergeant will be when we hand over the entire League of the Crimson Hand to the proper authorities.'

'Good ticket, Twinks.'

'So, though we've solved the murder—which wasn't a very hard rusk to chew—we now have another crime on our hands, don't we?'

'Do we?'

'The kidnapping of Laetitia Melmont.'

'Ah, yes,' said Blotto uneasily.

Seeing her brother's reaction, Twinks suggested encouragingly, 'I suppose we could just inform the police and let them get on with a Missing Persons inquiry…? While we get on with foiling the evil plans of the League of the Crimson Hand.'

But, as she had rather suspected, Blotto wouldn't dream of being party to such an idea. He knew the matrimonial risks of rescuing Laetitia Melmont, but in such a situation he was too much of a gentleman to consider his own interests. 'We can't do that, Twinks me old biscuit barrel. That poor girl was under my protection when she was abducted. It was my Lagonda that she was snaffled from.'

'But equally it was your Lagonda she stowed away in, so if we're looking for a balance of moral—'

Blotto raised a hand and his sister was obediently silent. 'No,' he said, rather magnificently. 'Laetitia was kidnapped on my watch. If I didn't do my best to rescue her, I'd feel the worst kind of bad tomato. Saving her must be my overriding priority. Once she's safe, then we'll turn our attentions to the League of the Crimson Hand.'

'Of course,' observed Twinks, 'it's quite possible that sorting out one of the problems will also sort out the other one. Two budgies with the same boomerang.'

'Sorry, Twinks, not on the same page as you...?'

Patiently his sister explained. 'There is a very strong likelihood, Blotto me old cigarette case, the people who kidnapped Laetitia Melmont were in fact members of the League of the Crimson Hand.'

'Toad-in-the-hole...'

'That's what I said to you when we found the Lagonda empty.'

'Yes, true, old pineapple. I'd forgotten that.'

'So tomorrow morning, soon as we've finished the Savoy brekker, we want to shift like a pair of cheetahs in spikes and find Davy ap Dafydd.'

'Said Davy ap Dafydd being the boddo with the next tattoo on his finger?'

'Give that pony a rosette!' said Twinks. 'You've bonged it right on the nose, Blotters.'

'Hmm...' Blotto's perfect brow furrowed beneath its thatch of fair hair. 'But how do we find the stencher?'

'Oh, come on, bro. Will Tyler did give us a pretty solid clue with his dying breath, didn't he?'

The clouds cleared on Blotto's brow. 'Of course! "The Three—" But The Three What?'

'You got any thoughts?' Twinks's question was pure politeness. Blotto rarely had.

'The Three Musketeers...?' he hazarded. 'The Three Rs...? The Three Cheers...? The Three-Piece Suit...?'

'We are looking for the name of a public house.'

'Ah. Tickey-tockey. You got any ideas, Twinks?'

'Well, the obvious ones, I suppose, would be The Three Castles, The Three Crowns, The Three Horseshoes and The Three Tuns. But I'm not sure any of those fit the pigeonhole.' Her alabaster brow wrinkled with the effort of memory. 'I'm sure there was another clue in Will Tyler's dying words...'

'All you told me he said was that he used to meet this Davy boddo in a pub called The Three Something.'

'No, there was more.' Her brow cleared. 'He said that the place was a hell-hole.'

'A lot of London pubs would be, I imagine. Full of people of the oikish classes. I don't think we'd meet many of our sort in that kind of place.'

'Certainly not dressed in full evening fig. But "hell-hole"... "Hell-hole",' she repeated. 'I was wondering whether it might be something to do with Cerberus. Do you know Cerberus, Blotto?'

'I'm not sure,' he replied cautiously. 'I'm a bit of an empty revolver when it comes to names. Was he at Eton?'

'No. He was the Guardian of the Underworld.'

'I thought they called them porters.'

'Porters?'

'Yes, those boddos who work on the Tube.'

'I said Underworld, not Underground, Blotto.'

'Ah. So this chap...Cerby...thing...guarded the Underworld...?'

'Yes. Or, in other words, hell. He guarded the hell-hole.'

'And what kind of a pineapple was he?'

'He was a dog.'

'Well, I'll be snickered, Twinks. Are you telling me that Will Tyler was shot by a dog? How did it get its paw round the trigger?'

His sister's patience was once again tested, but as ever it survived the challenge. 'The point about Cerberus was that he had three heads.'

Blotto let out a low whistle. 'Well, I'll be jugged like a hare! That'd be very nifty when you're out shooting—dog could retrieve three birds at the same time. Where can one buy one of these spoffingly useful beasts?'

'No, Blotto. You couldn't buy one. Cerberus is mythological.'

'Ah.' Her brother nodded as though he understood the word. 'Well, you wouldn't want to bring that into the house, would you? The servants might catch it.'

Not reacting to his words, Twinks continued with her reasoning. 'So Cerberus is a three-headed dog. Now if there happened to be in London a pub called The Three-Headed Dog...well, it'd be all creamy éclair, wouldn't it?'

'Good ticket,' said Blotto, as his sister flicked through the directory.

But for once one of her mental flashes failed to ignite. 'Oh dear, no coconuts being awarded here, I'm afraid. How mizzly! There isn't one.'

'That's a bit of a candle-snuffer.'

But Twinks was only momentarily cast down. Then she saw an entry that brought a new sparkle to her eye. 'Oh, splendissimo! There may not be a pub called The Three-Headed Dog, but there is one called The Three Feathers.'

'Is that good?' asked Blotto tentatively.

'It's more than good. It's goodissimo with dollops of cream.'

'Don't you see?'

'No.'

'Davy ap Dafydd is a Welsh name, isn't it?'

'Is it?'

'So of course he'd frequent a pub called The Three Feathers. Right, let's finish up these cocktails and then we're back to the East End to track down Davy ap Dafydd.'

'Now?' asked Blotto plaintively. 'I thought we were going to put away the bulk of the menu in the Grill first.'

'No, no. If we solve the case in time, we can have a light supper when we come back.'

'A light supper?' That held about as much appeal for Blotto as a salad. What he demanded from a meal was a large slab of meat, garnished with good solid English vegetables. And all that batting against counterfeit Chinamen had taken it out of him.

But he knew better than to try and change Twinks's mind when she had that determined set to her jaw. So he just poured the remains of his St Louis Steamhammer from shaker to glass and downed it in one.

When the lights stopped exploding in front of his eyes and the cocktail's aftershocks had subsided, Blotto asked his sister as they left the suite, 'Still not quite up to speed with you on this, Twinks...What is the connection between this Welsh boddo and The Three Feathers?'

'The Three Feathers is the heraldic symbol of the Prince of Wales.'

'Broken biscuits, Twinks...' Blotto was shocked. 'Are you saying the Royal Family are hand-in-glove with the League of the Crimson Hand?'

Chapter Fifteen

Spit and Sawdust

The Three Feathers public house was not in such a squalid part of London as Shanghai Billee's had been, but to Blotto and Twinks it still looked pretty murdy. The Lagonda had to drive through endless grimy terraces of houses which the Tawcesters would have considered too small to use as kennels, but where presumably oikish people managed to live, even with children. The buildings were cellars for the salt of the earth.

At the end of one such terrace stood their destination. The pub building seemed hunched over itself, like a poor man with a chest infection. The windows were uncurtained and yellow light trickled out on to the pavement. Creaking on its gallows, the inn sign featured three greyish feathers emerging from a crown which might once have been gold.

Blotto drew the Lagonda to a neat halt directly outside the entrance. There had been no opportunity to have repaired the slit in the fabric roof which had been made when Laetitia Melmont was abducted outside Shanghai Billee's. 'But I'm not going to don my worry-boots about that,' he told his sister. 'There nothing of value in the car, so it's quite safe.'

As they stood on the pavement outside The Three Feathers, Twinks became aware of what they were wearing. Dressed for dinner at the Savoy Grill, Blotto was in full boiled shirt, white tie and tails, while she wore a sleeveless, ankle-length number in eau-de-nil silk. A white mink stole protected her narrow shoulders, and the silver-sequined snood on her head exactly matched her small reticule.

'You don't you think we'll look out of place?' Twinks suggested tentatively.

'Oh, come on, Twinks, it is evening, after all. Surely even in a place like this boddos dress for dinner.'

This surmise, when they entered the pub, proved to be untrue. The salt of the earth, who appeared to have been sprinkled all round the bar by an overzealous waiter, were dressed in various shades of muddy brown and grey. They belonged to a species alien to the Tawcester family, people who went out to work every day. And even Blotto, who was very generous in his assessment of his fellow human beings, reckoned they were a scummy lot.

Nor did they seem pleased by the new arrivals. Ever polite, Blotto had ushered his sister into the pub ahead of himself, and at her entrance a total silence had fallen on the clientele. Jokes were stopped seconds before their punch-lines, dominoes suspended in mid-air, pint glasses replaced on sticky tables. Matches held up to light cigarettes were allowed to burn themselves out, as the pub's regulars glared at the apparitions in the doorway.

'Evening, all,' said Twinks, using the voice with which, every Christmas Day, she made her annual inquiry about the health of her maid's parents. 'No need to stand on ceremony with us.'

'No,' Blotto agreed. 'We're just ordinary greengages like you are. Just normal people nipping down the pub of an evening for a noggin of wallop.' He moved towards the bar and grinned his most boyish grin at the stony-faced landlord. 'Now what would you recommend, mine host?'

'Depends what you want to drink,' the man replied, reasonably enough.

'Well, I've just been drinking a rather splendid tincture called a St Louis Steamhammer. Don't suppose you could knock up one of those, could you?'

'No.'

'Oh, my sister was on a Cobbler's Awl. Any chance of mixing her one of those, me old pineapple?'

One might have thought that the landlord's face had reached its point of maximum glower, but this proved not to be the case. He raised his glower level by at least two degrees, as he said, ''Ere, you trying to pull my chain?'

'No, no. Last thing I'd want to do. Not that I can actually see your chain, anyway. Still, fair enough, if you don't stretch to cocktails. Probably not the demand for them in a place like this. And I'm sure my sister and I can make do with a dry white. Do you have a Château St Gilberton '04?'

'No.'

'Oh well, at a pinch I could settle for the '05. Do you have some of that on ice?'

'No.'

'Oh.'

'What're you rattling on about, anyway? I haven't understood a word you've said since you came in.'

'I was talking about wine.'

'Wine? In The Three Feathers?'

For the first time the silence in the bar was broken. The landlord's laugh was picked up slowly until the whole room rang with its contemptuous sound.

When the derision had died down sufficiently for him to be heard, the man behind the bar continued: 'This is a pub, not some poncy French restaurant.'

'Tickey-tockey,' said Blotto. 'But you do serve drinks?'

'Yes. That's what a pub does.'

'So what kind of drinks?'

'Mild, bitter, whisky, gin, brandy.'

'Oh, I think we'll both have large brandies, thank you. Now there's one I'm particularly partial to. When it comes to cognacs, though it's just from a small château, it's absolutely the lark's larynx. So if by any chance you've got a...' But a look from the landlord stopped Blotto from being more specific about the particular vintage of brandy he would have preferred.

After their outburst of merriment the pub's customers had reverted to suspicious silence. The noises made by the pouring of two drinks at the bar seemed suddenly very loud.

Twinks decided it was the moment for a frontal attack. As the landlord passed across their brandies, she flashed him her most dazzling smile. It was the same smile that had cut a swath through the entire Eton First Eleven at one Eton and Harrow match, leaving many of them with symptoms of grogginess, weak knees and embarrassingly vivid dreams for weeks afterwards.

But it wrought no change in the granite features of The Three Feathers' landlord. Twinks made her next assault vocally, using the honeyed tones which had once persuaded an Archbishop to do the Charleston. 'We are looking,' she susurrated, 'for a man called Davy ap Dafydd...'

So sharp was the intake of breath from every customer that The Three Feathers only just avoided becoming a vacuum. And the shock of the name even sent a minimal twitch across the impassive face of the landlord.

'Davy ap Dafydd?' he repeated.

'Who's asking for him?' a deep Welsh voice boomed from the recesses of the pub. Blotto and Twinks turned to see a huge man rising from his seat. He was dressed in fuzzy tweed and woolly gloves, and had such shaggy hair and such a heavy beard that his outline was as imprecise as a badly taken photograph.

'My name's Blotto,' announced Blotto in his usual open manner, but before he could compromise them by telling the truth, his sister cut in.

'We bring a message for you from Will Tyler,' she said.

The giant nodded and turned to the landlord. 'We'll go in the snug,' he growled, 'and if you catch anyone trying to eavesdrop...' He made an uncomfortably realistic throat-cutting gesture. The landlord nodded. 'And that goes for you too.'

With this threat Davy ap Dafydd led his two visitors through a door to the side of the counter. As he left, a slow rumble of apprehensive conversation started up again in the main bar. The Welshman sent two old ladies scuttering out of the snug with their bottles of milk stout and gestured for Blotto and Twinks to sit down.

The room in which they found themselves was snug only in the sense of being small. There was no cosiness about its dark discoloured panelling and it smelled as though behind its skirting boards many rats had lost the will to live.

While the Welsh giant settled himself, Twinks looked with frustration at the man's gloved hands. There was no chance of her surreptitiously noting the letters of the tattoo that she was sure lay beneath their woollen protection.

'Will Tyler...' said Davy ap Dafydd ruminatively. 'Will Tyler. Why didn't he approach me himself in the usual way?'

'Well,' replied Blotto, 'he's in a bit of a gluepot so far as that's concerned. You see, he's been—'

Once again Twinks intervened before any damage could be done. 'He had orders from someone higher up the chain of command that we should be the ones who got in touch with you.'

'That's strange.' The Welshman now sounded very suspicious. 'The whole point of the cell system is meant to be that each of us only has one contact.' He glowered at them. 'If I find out that you're up to something, I'll strangle the pair of you with my bare hands.'

While recognizing the benefit that baring his hands might bring her with regard to reading his tattoo, Twinks was also aware of the reality of his threat.

'And don't imagine that anyone in this pub would stand in my way,' the giant went on. 'They'd help me strangle you.

And they'd help me dispose of your bodies. They enjoy cutting things into little bits in The Three Feathers.'

He leered at them. Blotto opened his mouth to say something that Twinks knew would be chivalrous and fool-hardy, but she managed to get in first. Improvising wildly, she announced, 'When I said "someone higher up the chain of command", I meant "someone *very much* higher up the chain of command".'

Davy ap Dafydd peered at her from beneath the thatch of his eyebrows. ' "Very much higher"? How much higher?'

'As high as you like,' Twinks hazarded.

Her luck held. A low whistle escaped from the thickets of Davy ap Dafydd's beard. 'You mean...The One Whose Name Cannot Be Known...?'

'Yes, that's exactly who I mean,' Twinks replied dramatically. Then, for effect, she repeated, 'The One Whose Name Cannot Be Known.' And hoped to strengthen her position further by saying, 'The Crimson Thumb.'

Apparently impressed, the Welshman was silent for a moment. Then, disappointingly from Blotto and Twinks's point of view, he asked, 'Why should I believe you?'

That was actually, it had to be confessed, a rather good question. And not one to which even Twinks could come up with an immediate answer.

Her silence seemed only to fuel Davy ap Dafydd's suspicion. He flexed his huge hands inside their woollen gloves, as if in preparation for strangling. Blotto tensed, fairly confident that if it did come to violence, he was in with a good chance. Pity he'd left his cricket bat in the Lagonda, though.

He looked across at Twinks, to whom fortunately a new inspiration came at that moment. 'You believe me, Davy ap Dafydd,' she said evenly, 'because I can tell you what Will Tyler had tattooed on his little finger.'

This did seem to stop the Welshman in his progress towards strangulation. 'Oh yes? So what does he have tattooed there?'

Twinks opened her mouth to reply, but the giant raised a hand to stop her. 'The tattoos must not be spoken out loud. Write down what is written on Will Tyler's little finger.'

Twinks produced a small silver-jacketed notebook and a silver propelling pencil from her reticule and did as instructed. 'GGEC', she wrote, then tore out the sheet and passed it across. Davy ap Dafydd looked at the letters and grunted approval. For the moment—though who could say how long a moment?—the threat of strangulation was lifted.

'So what do you want from me?' he asked.

'We want the name of the person above you. The Letter-Bearer of the Middle Finger.'

The Welshman's resistance seemed to have crumbled. In the voice of an automaton, he announced, 'The Letter-Bearer of the Middle Finger is Gerhardt Sachs.'

'And how do you contact him?'

Machine-like, Davy ap Dafydd replied, 'I always meet him at Croydon Aerodrome.'

'How do you know when to meet?'

'He puts an encoded message in the Personal Column of the *Daily Bugle*.'

'Do you meet at Croydon Aerodrome because Gerhardt Sachs flies in there?'

'Yes.'

'And where does he fly in from? From some Continental city?'

'No. He flies in from within the British Isles.'

'Where?'

'Somewhere I know well. Gerhardt Sachs is based in—'

But Davy ap Dafydd did not manage to articulate the location. He suffered the same fate as Will Tyler had done when about to release vital information. The sound of a gunshot coincided with the shattering of glass and a bullet-hole appeared in the giant's forehead. He slumped forward. Dead.

Blotto was instantly on his feet. 'If I'm quick, I'll catch the stencher who's done this!'

'You go!' said Twinks. 'I'll just check what Davy ap Dafydd has tattooed on his hand.'

As her brother shot out of the snug, Twinks removed the dead giant's right-hand glove.

On his ring finger were tattooed the letters: 'LLRA'. Twinks rushed out into the street, just as the door from The Three Feathers' main bar opened to reveal the curious faces of the landlord and most of his customers.

She found Blotto standing on the pavement, with the saddest expression she had ever seen on his face.

'What's up, old pineapple? You look like a squirrel who's had his last nut nicked just before the onset of winter.'

'Look.' He pointed bleakly into the road. Where there was nothing to see. Least of all an extremely beautiful Lagonda.

Blotto's jaw line set in an uncharacteristic expression of fury. He'd got into this investigation because the Dowager Duchess of Melmont had been murdered. Laetitia's abduction had given him an extra incentive. But now the stenchers had stolen his Lagonda the case had become personal.

Chapter Sixteen

The Sky's the Limit!

'Where will they have taken it?' Blotto asked despairingly. 'Rodents! I'll never be able to look Corky Froggett in the face again. It'll be bad enough for him to be hanged for a murder he didn't commit. A man with the sterling qualities of Corky'll get over that, but he'll never survive the loss of the Lag. He loves that car like a mother sheep loves her favourite yew tree.'

'I think you mean ewe lamb, Blotto.'

'Oh yes. All right, tickey-tockey. But where are we going to start looking for the Lag? We don't have a clue where the thieving bad tomato has taken it.'

'Oh, but we do.'

Blotto looked curiously at his sister, then was suddenly aware that behind her the sullen regulars of The Three Feathers were pouring out on to the street. The expressions on their oikish faces were far from philanthropic.

'Tell me later, Twinks. I think right now we need to make ourselves as scarce as a lawyer's conscience.'

His sister turned to take in the advancing mob, then instantly pushed two fingers into her dainty mouth and let out a whistle that would have shattered wineglasses (had there been any wineglasses in the vicinity of The Three Feathers, which, as their inquiries at the bar had proved, there weren't).

The noise had the effect of stopping the vengeful mob in their tracks. Only for a second, but in that second a taxi had appeared beside Blotto and Twinks and they had bundled themselves into it.

'Croydon Aerodrome,' Twinks told the cabbie, 'and drive like a cheetah on spikes!'

Blotto once again found himself lost in admiration for another of his sister's skills. 'How did you do it, Twinks? How did you know there'd be a cab there?'

'Self-belief,' Twinks replied. 'It's a trait I've inherited from our mother. Can you imagine any cabbie in London daring not to appear if the Mater whistled?'

Blotto was forced to admit that he couldn't. There was a silence between them, then he said, 'Not much fun being a Letter-Bearer for the League of the Crimson Hand, is it? Because as soon as you reach the point of uncaging the ferrets about something really important, you get coffinated.'

'It does seem to be a hazard of the profession, yes.'

'Mm. Incidentally, Twinks me old muffin...Why are we going to Croydon Aerodrome?'

'Because I'll lay a guinea to a groat that that's where we'll find your Lagonda.'

'Toad-in-the-hole...' murmured Blotto, impressed and excited. Then, after a silence, he asked, 'What makes you think that, old greengage?'

'Because of the clues that Davy ap Dafydd gave us.'

'Oh yes. Right. Of course. What clues?'

'The obvious ones,' Twinks replied patiently. 'He said he always met Gerhardt Sachs at Croydon Aerodrome.'

'Yes, but he said it involved having small ads printed in the *Daily Bugle*. Surely you haven't had time to do that since we've left the pub, have you?' It seemed unlikely, but Blotto had long since learned not to underestimate his sister's skills.

'No, you prize cauliflower, of course I haven't. But I've got a hunch...'

'Have you? It doesn't show. I mean, I'm sure I'd have noticed it when we played together as children if—'

'No, Blotters, not that kind of hunch. I mean I've got an instinct that we're on the right track. I'm sure the next stage of our investigation lies at Croydon Aerodrome.'

'Oh.' He had to admit to a little disappointment. He had been expecting Twinks to present him with a finely wrought chain of logic, which would prove irrefutably that the killer of Davy ap Dafydd—probably the same spoffing stencher who'd had the temerity to steal the Lagonda—was on his way to Croydon Aerodrome. But all she'd come up with was an *instinct*. Well, anyone could have an instinct. Blotto himself even had instincts from time to time. Though it had to be said that his track record for having instincts that were *right* was not nearly as impressive as his sister's.

Still, Blotto was comforted by the possibility of being reunited with his Lagonda.

Twinks appeared to know her way around Croydon Aerodrome. She moved confidently through the pillared space of the main booking hall to an information desk, quickly scribbled a note and handed it to the uniformed woman behind the counter. 'Tell him we'll be in the cocktail lounge,' she announced, and led her slightly bewildered brother to that destination.

Sadly, St Louis Steamhammers hadn't reached from the Savoy to the suburban outskirts of Croydon, so they contented themselves with gin and tonics. When they were seated with their drinks, Blotto asked, 'So who is this boddo you've fixed to rendezvous with?'

'Perfectly amiable greengage called Jerome Handsomely.'

'Where'd you meet him?'

'At a ball.' Twinks shrugged her slender shoulders.

'Anything special I should know about him?'

'No, don't think so. He's a pilot.' The azure eyes were screwed up in an effort of recollection. 'Oh yes, and he's in love with me.'

That doesn't narrow it down much, thought Blotto. Every spoffing man his sister met seemed to fall in love with her. The unperforated stamps in the collection were the ones who didn't.

In a matter of moments Jerome Handsomely was with them. As he walked in he seemed to take over the entire cocktail lounge. Every eye instantly homed in on him. He was very tall, taller even than Blotto, which must have put him round the six-six mark. He had wavy black hair which he wore almost foppishly long, a luxuriant black moustache, pale skin and startlingly pale blue eyes. He wore jodhpurs and riding boots, and above the waist a sheepskin-lined leather blouson over a khaki shirt, at whose open neck fluttered a white silk scarf. From one nonchalant hand dangled a leather pilot's helmet and a pair of aviator goggles.

'Twinks!' he cried in a voice which had not scaled the heights of Eton or Harrow, but had been to a perfectly decent minor public school for the terminally unacademic. 'Gosh, aren't you looking the absolute box of chocs! Just the sight of you flattens me like a whizzbang! I'm surprised vital parts of me aren't scattered all over the lounge.'

Twinks of course remained seated during this encomium, but Blotto had risen politely to his feet, and for the first time Jerome Handsomely seemed aware of his presence. And he wasn't best pleased with what he saw. 'I say, who's the tinkety-tonker? I must say I regard this as a bit beyond the barbed wire, Twinks. Summoning me to meet you when you're sugaring away over G and Ts with some smarmed-up lounge-leech.'

Not giving Twinks time to offer any explanation, Jerome Handsomely turned on Blotto. 'Now listen, you bally stopcock-twiddler! The view I take of your frattering with Twinks is dimmer than a mole's in a coal-hole. And I demand satisfaction! I know duelling's illegal these days, but we can find a crumpety corner of the airfield and do the business. To the death, of course! You can have the choice of weapons, you chicken-livered switch-clicker!'

Blotto said, 'Erm,' and looked to Twinks for support.

'Jerome,' she announced gracefully, 'I don't believe you've met my brother Blotto.'

'Ah. Brother. Brother clearly in vision at ten o'clock.' A genteel smile took over the pilot's face, as he reached his hand across. 'Absolutely snuffled-up to meet you, me old cheese straw.'

'Tickey-tockey to meet you too,' said Blotto, taking the proffered hand.

Polite relations restored, Jerome Handsomely turned back to Twinks. 'Have you brought your brother along as a witness?'

'A witness to what?'

'Your agreeing to you and me getting meshed. Your waving the starter's flag on our engagement.'

Twinks smiled apologetically. 'Sorry, Jerome. I'm afraid my answer to that is the same as it has ever been.'

The pilot looked crushed. 'Oh, wingless biplanes!' he cried. 'But, Twinks, you know I love you with all the trimmings, even down to the game chips and blackcurrant jelly.'

'I know you do, Jerome.'

His pale brow darkened. 'There isn't *another*, is there? There isn't another slimer who's been slipping you the soft centres?'

'No. There is no one else in my life of a romantic nature.'

'But, mind you, every man she meets falls for her like a giraffe on an ice rink.' Blotto thought he ought to mention that fact, but the look Jerome Handsomely turned on him suggested it might not have been such a good idea, after all.

'Look, Twinks,' the pilot began despairingly, 'I love you more than a steeplechaser loves his bran. I'd lay down my life for you as readily as a lizard glumphs down a fly. Would that help, Twinks? Would it help if I laid my life down for you?'

'I don't really think it would help at all, Jerome. You're going to be much more use to me alive than you would be dead.'

'Oh.' He was cast down for a moment. Clearly the thought of laying down his life had rather appealed to him, and it would take a moment for him to come to terms with being refused permission. But, after a moment of self-reconciliation, his expression brightened. 'So, Twinks, you are saying that there is something you want me to do for you?'

'There certainly is.'

'Oh, giant aspidistras! That's booming news! What is it?' A new exciting thought came to him. 'Is it something hazardous? Something which might possibly lead to my laying down my life for you in the attempt?'

'I don't think it need be, no.' At her words Jerome Handsomely looked so miserable that Twinks hastened to reassure him. 'But it might well be that dangerous, yes.'

Instantly cheered, he demanded to know what service it was she required of him. Anything. Anything. And he reiterated that if the task did actually involve his laying down his life…well, that would be a real bonus.

Twinks moved quickly to practicalities. 'We are looking for a man called Gerhardt Sachs. We believe he frequently flies into Croydon Aerodrome, though we don't know in what capacity. But if we could track him down, it would be pure creamy éclair.'

'When you say he "flies in", me old iced bun…do you mean the poached egg's a pilot?'

'He might be. We don't know.'

'Because I know most of the away-chockers who've got pilot's licences around this tea chest, and the name doesn't tickle my memory glands.'

'Maybe he uses another name…?' Twinks suggested.

'Booming good notion! "Gerhardt Sachs" might not be top of the favourite names round Croydon Aerodrome after the last dust-up in Europe.'

'That's what I was thinking,' Twinks agreed.

'Do you know what the sausage-muncher looks like?' asked Jerome.

'Afraid we don't. Never seen him.'

'That's a bit of a knuckle-cracker. Do we have any other clues as to how to spot the target?'

'Well…' said Blotto, who had been silent for rather a long time. 'The stencher might have driven here in a stolen Lagonda.'

'Great dithering dragonflies!' exclaimed Jerome Handsomely. 'If you'd said that straight away, I could have taken you there quicker than a doctor's bill. Come with me!'

'You can take us to Gerhardt Sachs?' asked Twinks.

'If he's still here, yes. But his crate was being prepped, so he may have twanged off the tarmac by now.'

'But can you take us straight to my Lagonda?' asked Blotto, who had different priorities from his sister.

'Quick as a whizzbang's wake,' asserted Jerome Handsomely. 'Just take my lead in the tango.'

As the pilot strode off, again followed by every eye in the cocktail lounge, Blotto murmured, 'Toad-in-the-hole, Twinks. That boddo's slang's a tough rusk to chew, isn't it?'

'Yes, Blotto me old biscuit barrel, greengages who've been through the Royal Flying Corps seem virtually to have invented a language of their own.'

'Well, it's a bit of a candle-snuffer. Why can't he uncage the ferrets in normal English like you and me, Twinks me old banana box?'

Chapter Seventeen

Into Thin Air

Jerome Handsomely strode through life as if he always knew where he was going, and that was the way he swept through Croydon Aerodrome with Blotto and Twinks in his wake. Avoiding the marked routes for paying travellers, he ushered them through door after door marked 'Private' and they were soon out by the hangars that didn't belong to commercial airlines. There it was that wealthy daredevils parked their crates.

There wasn't much activity, most of the planes being tucked up for the night in their hangars. But the throbbing of a propeller drew their attention to a small plane out on the tarmac. Its undercarriage lights were on, and it appeared to be readying for take-off.

'Great repeating radishes!' cried Jerome Handsomely. 'It's a Frimmelstopf Fliegflügel!'

'A what?' asked Twinks.

'Latest technology from the sausage-munchers. Two-seater—

booming crate! Don't like their crocking politics and I've had a lifelong aversion to sauerkraut, but when it comes to engineering, they paddle a different canoe. You see, it's only got one wing.'

'Oh,' said Blotto, 'isn't that a bit awkward?'

'In what way, me old poached egg?'

'Well, doesn't the spotting thing fly round in circles? I mean, that's what happens when you're out shooting. You wing a bird and it kind of spirals down in a—'

'No, no,' Jerome Handsomely interrupted. 'It's only got one wing that goes right across. As opposed to two, which is what a biplane has.'

'Ah.' Blotto appeared to lose interest.

'But in that kite over there, Jerome,' asked Twinks excitedly, 'do you believe that Gerhardt Sachs is the pilot?'

'It'd match the carpet, wouldn't it, for him to have a Frimmelstopf Fliegflügel...given his name?'

'Yes, but...' Twinks suddenly realized that Blotto was no longer with them. He'd drifted away and was looking into the middle distance. On his face was a look popularized in stained-glass windows by saints who have just been vouchsafed a private glimpse of the Almighty.

'Blotto, Blotto, what is it?'

He pointed. His sister moved closer, to a position where she could see, beyond the Frimmelstopf Fliegflügel, the sight that had beatified her brother's features. It was the Lagonda.

'Well,' she said, 'that proves there's a connection between The Three Feathers and Croydon Aerodrome. I'd lay a guinea to a groat that the pilot of that plane is Gerhardt Sachs.'

As she said the words, the engine note from the Frimmelstopf Fliegflügel changed and they saw the plane beginning to move towards the runway.

'Great slithering sea snakes!' said Jerome Handsomely. 'We'll catch the slimer. Quick! My crate's prepped and as ready to go as a cougar who's just dined off a coiled spring.' He started to run towards the only other plane on the tarmac, an Accrington-Murphy Painted Lady Biplane.

Twinks was about to follow him when she saw that Blotto was hurrying in the other direction. 'Where are you going?'

'My Lagonda,' he replied almost pathetically.

'But we've got to follow Gerhardt Sachs!'

'I'll follow him in the Lagonda,' her brother insisted.

'Blotters, the Lag is a wonderful car. It can do many things, but the one thing it can't do is fly.'

'But I could follow the stencher on the roads.'

'Which would be all fine and sprightly, if he followed the line of the roads. Which I think he's very unlikely to do.'

Reluctantly, Blotto accepted the force of her argument and the two of them ran, resplendent in their evening wear, towards Jerome Handsomely's Accrington-Murphy Painted Lady Biplane. He already had the propeller turning as they clambered up and into the narrow cockpit. Ahead of them on the tarmac they could see the tail-lights of the Frimmelstopf Fliegflügel as it lifted off the runway.

'Right, Jerome,' Twinks commanded, 'follow that plane!'

Chapter Eighteen

Aerial Pursuit

'I'd have thought,' said Blotto pensively after they had been flying for about ten minutes, 'that it'd be jolly difficult to follow another plane without the boddo driving the spoffing thing knowing that he was being followed. I mean, the sky's quite a big place, isn't it? And dashed empty. So there's not much to hide behind except the odd cloud.'

'Ah yes,' the pilot replied. 'But what you have to take into account, me old propeller-winder, is that the sausage-muncher ahead of us doesn't suspect that he's being followed.'

'Wouldn't he have seen you taking off?'

'No, I was too far behind. And I didn't have any of my lights on when I twanged my crate off the tarmac. What's more, I've switched off all my radio proggers and plumbing, so the tinkety-tonker won't be able to detect us that way.'

'Isn't that rather dangerous?' asked Twinks.

'Of course it is! But life without danger is like a mince pie with no brandy butter. Taking off in a crate when you haven't got at least an even chance of not coming back is about as exciting as a game of patience in a girls' dormitory. And by the way, Twinks, you know you only have to say the booming word and I'll happily lay down my life for you.'

'You did mention that, yes.'

'Well, it's still a good offer. Just say the word and I'll be absolutely snuffled-up to do it. Piece of cake caning yourself when you're up in a crate. Just take your hands off the helmrod and a few minutes later you're Pilot Flambé in a field. If you'd like me to do, it, me old iced bun...' He took his hands off the instruments by way of demonstration.

'No!' Twinks's shriek did at least make him once again take hold of the controls. 'There's something you're not taking into account, Jerome.'

'Great dithering dragonflies! What is it?'

'While you would be so generously laying down your life for me...'

'Yes?'

'...you would also be laying down two other people's lives as well. It wouldn't just be Pilot Flambé in a field. It'd be Blotto and Twinks Flambés in a field too. So your laying down your life for me would be as much use as a tail-curler to a Manx cat.'

'Ah, hadn't thought of that particular knuckle-cracker. Booming good point, Twinks. Have to save laying down my life for you till a more crumpety occasion.'

'If you wouldn't mind, Jerome me old Labrador. I think at the moment you're much more use to me with your life kept tinkling on rather than being laid down.'

The pilot acknowledged the wisdom of her reply by nodding his head and saying, 'Trucky-trockle.'

'Tickey-tockey,' Blotto confirmed.

There was a silence. They all looked ahead, eyes fixed on the distant red pin-spots of the Frimmelstopf Fliegflügel. The fog-muffled lights of London had been left behind them, but though the night was now clear, the darkness prevented them from seeing the beautiful English countryside over which they were flying.

'Without your instruments,' asked Twinks, 'have you any idea in which direction we're flying?'

'We're going more or less due west.'

'How do you know that?'

Jerome Handsomely's eyes flicked up to the sky above him. 'Stars, Twinks. The oldest navigation aid of them all. If it's good enough for Jason and his booming Argonauts, then it ticks the clock for me too.'

Twinks too looked up. The stars seemed clearer than they ever had before. She felt a little surge of romantic soppiness. Thank goodness Blotto was there. She was in the kind of mood when, if alone with Jerome Handsomely, she could possibly even succumb to his blandishments. He was a dashed tasty slice of redcurrant cheesecake, after all.

She looked across at her brother. He was pensive, not to say downright melancholic. Twinks didn't need to ask what was gnawing away at him. It was the thought of his Lagonda and whether it'd be safe at Croydon Aerodrome or whether some other frightful stencher from the League of the Crimson Hand was likely to steal it again.

She was about to say something reassuring, but was stopped by Jerome Handsomely announcing, 'Our sausage-muncher's preparing to land his kite.'

Blotto and Twinks looked ahead and saw that the taillights of the Frimmelstopf Fliegflügel were indeed descending. 'What are you going to do, Jerome?' asked Twinks.

'See where the tinkety-tonker lands. If it's at a big commercial aerodrome, then giant aspidistras! I can land there too and no one'll think it's odd. If it's on a private landing strip, that could be more of a knuckle-cracker.'

'Why?' asked Blotto.

'Because,' his sister explained patiently, 'we'll be seen arriving there, and Gerhardt Sachs will know that he's being followed.'

'Ah, good ticket.'

'The sausage-muncher's circling,' Jerome Handsomely observed. 'He'll be tickling the tarmac soon.' A slight adjustment to the controls caused his Accrington-Murphy Painted Lady Biplane to mirror the spiralling movements of the Frimmelstopf Fliegflügel, but at a much greater height.

'Not going to lose sight of the stencher, are we?' asked Blotto.

'No,' the pilot reassured him. 'Even if we do lose sight of him, there's no way that away-chocker's going to land his crate on an unlit airstrip. That'd be a booming certain recipe for Pilot Flambé. The switch-clickers he's visiting will have lit up the target area for him, and we'll see that, even if we can't see him.'

As he spoke the words, a visual confirmation of them appeared. Out of the murk beneath, Blotto and Twinks could see a small rectangle of lights, whose glow illuminated the frontage of a very large country house.

'Oh, wingless biplanes!' said Jerome Handsomely. 'The bally stopcock-twiddler *is* landing on a private airstrip. If I follow suit, that'd be announcing our arrival with a booming great fanfare. Have to move to Plan B—or even Plan C.'

'Have you got a Plan B and a Plan C?' asked Blotto cautiously.

'Trucky-trockle, never leave home without them. Come to that, I've also always got a Plan D.'

'What's that?'

'Laying down my life for Twinks.'

'Yes,' said the object of his devotion, 'but we've already established that now isn't quite the moment to put Plan D into action.'

He saluted her. 'Order received and understood.' Then he looked down to the rectangle of light beneath them. 'Great dithering dragonflies! The Frimmelstopf Fliegflügel has landed!'

'So what are your Plans B and C?' asked Blotto after a moment of silence.

'Plan B is: we find the nearest commercial aerodrome, tickle the tarmac there and then try to work our way back here.'

'And Plan C?' asked Twinks.

'Plan C does come with a booming great risk attached.'

Blotto's eyes gleamed. 'I like it already. What do we do?'

'Well, the knuckle-cracker with it so far as I'm concerned is that the scheme doesn't involve me in any dust-up that may lie ahead. It'd be just you two facing whatever dangers these tinkety-tonkers might come up with.'

'That's grandissimo with us, Jerome. Blotto and I are used to facing danger together.'

'Hoopee-doopee!' her brother agreed. 'So tell us what your Plan C is.'

'Right. I keep this crate circling over the landing strip and then you two parachute down.'

'Toad-in-the-hole!' said Blotto.

'That'll be pure creamy éclair!' said Twinks.

'Have either of you parachuted before?' asked Jerome Handsomely.

They both admitted that they hadn't. 'But it can't be too hard a rusk to chew,' said Blotto. 'I mean, gravity does most of the work, doesn't it?'

'Ye-es. But there are still a few tips I ought to give you.'

'Well, come on, Jerome me old greengage, uncage the ferrets.'

So the pilot passed on the basics of parachuting to them while they struggled in the confined space to attach their parachute packs. 'The most important thing,' he concluded, 'is that you keep that lighted airstrip in sight and aim for it. Those lights are going to be your fixed point. If you don't come down somewhere near there things could get pretty crocking for you. So keep that in sight, otherwise you could end up on a mountainside or stuck in a tree.'

'Good ticket,' said Blotto.

Getting out of the Accrington-Murphy Painted Lady Biplane was not the easiest manoeuvre the brother and sister had ever attempted, but they managed it. Jumping free, they followed Jerome Handsomely's instructions, counting to five and then pulling the ripcords of their parachutes. Soon they were floating through the tingling night air, still resplendent in their dinner wear.

'Oh, what larks!' murmured Twinks ecstatically.

At that moment the rectangle of lights which showed their destination were all extinguished.

'Oh, larksissimo!' cried a joyous Twinks.

Chapter Nineteen

The Black Mountains

The night through which they floated was blacker than Beluga caviar. Neither Blotto nor Twinks had a clue where they were, but the rush of air as they descended gave them a sensation of gleeful irresponsibility. Both thought idly that they should perhaps have asked Jerome Handsomely for a pointer to their geographical location, but it didn't seem that important.

Their only mild worry was that, not knowing when they were about to hit the ground, they didn't know when to brace themselves for the impact. Still, they thought, what's a broken leg? They'd both sustained them on occasion in hunting accidents and yes, they were a bore, but survivable. Though they did realize that broken limbs might render them a little less efficient in their approaching confrontation with Gerhardt Sachs...and maybe with other members of the League of the Crimson Hand.

Jerome had warned them of the dangers of trees, but as it turned out trees were their salvation. The crackle of the bare branches through which they fell was their first clue to how close to the ground they were. And the speed with which the crackling noises mounted told them they were going far too fast for safety. Maybe two broken legs, they both thought with the stoicism inculcated in them by their mother's inattention to her children's injuries.

But, as the ropes of their parachutes began to tangle in the trees, their descent slowed. Their fall, rather than their legs, had been broken. Blotto and Twinks ended up dangling from the branches, bobbing gently up and down, their feet some six inches off the ground. They released their harnesses, dropped down and adjusted their clothing. Though she could see very little, Twinks instinctively drew a powder compact from her reticule and repaired her make-up. Blotto straightened his white tie and flicked the tails of his coat. They both once again looked perfectly accoutred for dinner at the Savoy.

But of course their immediate task was a less comfortable one than that. They had to find Gerhardt Sachs and check what was tattooed on his middle finger. And if their experience with the other Letter-Bearers was anything to go by, he might well resist their attentions.

Blotto and Twinks's eyes were now adjusting to the darkness and they began to have a vague sense of the space around them. What they saw told them how very lucky they'd been in their landing. There were very few trees in the undulating landscape, but a good few exposed crags. A landing on one of them would have been a lot less welcoming than their descent through the branches.

Though they could see the blurred outlines of a few sheep, there was no sign of any human habitation. 'Where the strawberries are we, Twinks me old biscuit barrel?' asked Blotto. 'Have you got a mouse squeak of an idea?'

'Well, given the direction in which we were flying, and the outline of the landscape here, I'd say we were in the Black Mountains.'

'Ah, Black Mountains,' echoed Blotto. Then after a moment he said, 'And where are they?'

'Wales. On the Welsh-English border.'

'Oh. I've never been to Wales.'

'I know that, Blotto.'

'Never seen the necessity.'

'No.'

'And here I am—in Wales.'

'Yes.'

'Well, I'll be jugged like a hare...' He looked at the darkened countryside around him. 'So what do we do now, Twinks? Choose a direction and start walking in it?'

'No, we walk towards the big house where Gerhardt Sachs landed.'

'Good ticket. Only gluepot there is: we don't know which direction it's in.'

'Yes, we do.' Twinks pointed out a slender and determined arm.

'But how do you know that's where it is?'

'I noticed as we were parachuting down.'

'How? I kept spinning around as if I was seriously wobbulated. I've no idea whether the house is east, west or sideways.'

'I kept taking bearings on the stars, like Jerome did.'

'Toad-in-the-hole, Twinks! You are quite a girl. Once again I find myself asking how all that brain manages to fit into such a tiny cranium without spilling out your ears. Do you have a spare tank hidden somewhere inside your body for all the extra cells?'

His sister let out a tinkling laugh. 'Don't talk such toffee, Blotto. Come on, let's find Gerhardt Sachs.'

Needless to say, Twinks's sense of direction was impeccably accurate, and they soon found themselves outside a high brick wall enclosing an estate. They were a little footsore by now. The muddy terrain had been very tough on Twinks's silver slippers, and not much kinder to Blotto's patent leather evening shoes.

'You reckon it was in here that the Frimmelstopf Fliegflügel landed?' asked Blotto in a hoarse whisper.

'I'd put my last solitary sapphire on it,' Twinks replied.

'So what do we do—walk round until we find the spoffing entrance?'

'I think that could be asking for trouble, Blotto me old gumdrop. If this place is guarded—and if I had another sapphire left, I'd put that on the fact that it is—the guards are going to be concentrated by the gates. We'll do better getting in over the wall.'

'The old "convenient tree" routine?'

'Exactly.'

Blotto looked along the wall in each direction. Now fully adjusted to the darkness, his eyes could see a lot further. 'Look!' He pointed triumphantly. 'A convenient tree!'

It was a matter of moments for them to reach the tree, for Blotto to shin up it, reach a hand down to give his sister a lift, and for both of them to straddle the top of the wall and drop down inside the estate.

They could see now that Twinks's surmise had been correct. Before them rose the huge house they had glimpsed from the sky. And in front of it was an airstrip on which stood Gerhardt Sachs's Frimmelstopf Fliegflügel.

'Hoopee-doopee!' whispered a delighted Blotto. 'You've found it! Give that pony a rosette! So what do we do now, Twinks?'

'We go up to the house. But we must be as silent as a butler's shoes. I'm pretty sure there are guards around this place.'

As if to provide a helpful illustration to her words, at that moment they heard the approach of heavy feet and shrank into the shadows of the wall until a uniformed man with a gun on his shoulder had walked past them.

Brother and sister waited a few moments before moving cautiously ahead. They were fortunate, in that the garden was formally laid out with walls and hedges, ideal for lurking and scuttling behind.

They lurked and scuttled their way up to the house. Through the gloaming they could see more uniformed guards at the front entrance, so they lurked and scuttled a bit more round to the side. They trod through the soft earth of flowerbeds up against the walls, which, as well as being quieter, were easier on their sore feet. And each time they passed a window, Blotto bobbed up to take a peek inside.

For the first four windows his scrutiny was unrewarded. Thick curtains were closed tight, and no chink of light escaped them.

But on the fifth window, the curtains had been incompletely drawn, leaving a small triangle of light at the bottom through which Blotto could look into the room.

The first thing he saw was Laetitia Melmont.

Though it was the middle of the night, she was dressed. Not in the clothes in which he had last seen her on their journey to London, but in a kind of shapeless dark blue overall, on the front of which, against her ironing-board chest, was the embroidered outline of a Crimson Hand. She had in her hand what looked like a prayer book, which she was reading with great concentration.

Around one of her wrists was a handcuff, from which a chain ran to a large metal radiator, where it was attached by a padlock.

'Toad-in-the-hole,' murmured Blotto to his sister. 'Now we know we're on the right track.'

'You're bong on the nose there, Blotto. Do you reckon we'll be able to rescue the poor greengage?'

'Of course we will. A job like this is absolutely my size of pyjamas.'

He tested the security of the window. If he had to break the glass, he would, but he knew doing that would risk making a noise which might alert Laetitia's captors. If he could slide up the sash window in the conventional way, that would be a lot safer.

Blotto was in luck. The guards from the League of the Crimson Hand must have reckoned that the chain would prevent their prisoner getting anywhere near the window, so they hadn't bothered to lock it. By exerting upward pressure on the top of the lower part, Blotto had the satisfaction of feeling it move, and he continued to push.

The noise alerted Laetitia. She looked up from her book with an expression of horror, which melted into ecstasy when she saw who it was entering the room.

'Blotto!' she cried, fortunately at a lower level of decibels than she usually favoured. 'You've come to rescue me! To show your love for me!'

'Oh, biscuits!' said Blotto under his breath. He'd forgotten how such an act of chivalry was likely to be interpreted by the 'the Snitterings Ironing-Board'. To cover his embarrassment, he turned to help Twinks up over the sill into the room.

His sister immediately put a finger to her lips to silence further effusions from Laetitia Melmont. 'We'll get you free, but we must be as silent as a butler's shoes. While we release you, you must uncage the ferrets—very quietly, though—about how you came to be here and what kind of stenchers we're up against.'

'Righty-ho,' said Laetitia.

'Just one thing, Twinks me old biscuit barrel...How're we going to free her from this spoffing chain? I'd happily have a pop at it with my bare teeth, but I'm not sure that I'd win any coconuts.'

'Don't worry, Blotto, I've got a file in my reticule.'

'Well, that's extremely fizzulating news. You really are the lark's larynx, you know, Twinks.'

'I do my best.' She reached into her reticule and produced the file, with which her brother immediately began to attack Laetitia's chain. A look at the sturdiness of the handcuff on her wrist told him he wasn't going to get through that, so he started filing through the link nearest to it.

'Oh, Blotto,' purred Laetitia, 'it is so good to feel you so close to me.'

Broken biscuits, he thought, it's going to be very sticky going getting out of this particular gluepot.

But fortunately his sister intervened before he was subjected to any more amorous displays. 'Shift your shimmy, Laetitia. Tell us everything that happened from the moment you were snatched outside Shanghai Billee's.'

Laetitia Melmont did as she was told, with difficulty keeping her natural Master of Foxhounds voice to a low level. She had been taken from the Lagonda in Limehouse by a gang of what she had assumed to be Chinamen—though what Blotto and Twinks now knew to have been members of the League of the Crimson Hand in disguise. She had been bundled into a nearby car and driven all the way to where they were now, which she informed them was called Llanystwyth House. And she confirmed Twinks's surmise that it was set in the Black Mountains.

Her captors had not ill-treated her, though she had been left in no doubt that they weren't about to set her free. Her food was brought and she was escorted to the bathroom by uniformed guards who would not allow themselves to be engaged in any kind of conversation. The only person in Llanystwyth House she could identify by name was a man called Wellborough Choat, who either owned or was in charge of the place. He had questioned her a few times since she'd been there, asking about the set-up at Snitterings and also the nature of her association with Devereux and Honoria Lyminster.

'Rodents!' said Blotto. 'That means the stenchers are on to us.'

'This man Choat,' asked Twinks, 'did you happen to notice whether he has a tattoo on his hand?'

'I couldn't tell you, I'm afraid. He's been wearing gloves every time he's come to see me.'

Twinks nodded thoughtfully. The man might have been wearing the gloves deliberately, like Davy ap Dafydd, to hide the tattoo. Maybe Wellborough Choat was the Letter-bearer of the Index Finger—? And if Gerhardt Sachs really was the Letter-Bearer of the Middle Finger, then right there in Llanystwyth House lay all the information they required to take them to the Crimson Thumb himself. She tried to repress the surge of excitement the thought gave her. Twinks never liked counting her blue tits before they were born.

'Hoopee-doopee!' said Blotto as he released the chain holding Laetitia. 'Now you're as free as an untethered Zeppelin. But I'm afraid you're stuck with that spoffing great bracelet till we can find a key for it.'

'I can't thank you enough, Blotto. Particularly because I know that everything you do for me is done because you love me.'

'Oh...er...um,' was all he could say, even though he knew that Laetitia Melmont would regard his inarticulacy as even more proof of his devotion.

'Well, come on, Blotto,' said Twinks. 'We'd better put a jumping cracker under it and beard these stenchers in their murdy den.'

'Am I coming with you?' asked Laetitia.

'No,' Twinks replied firmly. 'You stay here, just in case someone comes in, finds you gone and gets a whiff that the Stilton's iffy. And tuck the end of the chain into the handcuff so that it looks as if you're still attached to the radiator.'

'Oh, I do want to come with you. The thought of Blotto risking his life for me and me not seeing—'

'You stay here!' Twinks used the voice with which her mother had stopped the beasts in mid-pounce during her tiger-shooting days. 'Read your book.'

Laetitia Melmont looked so downcast that Blotto couldn't stop himself from asking tenderly, 'What is it you're reading, me old gumboil?'

She looked up at him, her eyes brimming with gratitude. 'St Thomas Aquinas,' she replied.

'Ah.' Blotto nodded. 'Book about horses.'

'What?'

'"Equine". Means "to do with horses". From the Latin. I learned that at school.'

'No, Blotto, it's—'

But Laetitia was once again interrupted by Twinks. 'Come on, Blotto. It's time for another confrontation with the League of the Crimson Hand!'

Chapter Twenty

Confrontation at Llanystwyth House

As Blotto and Twinks crept through the corridors of Llanystwyth House, there was no sign of any guards. Maybe Wellborough Choat was so confident that no one could penetrate his inner sanctum that he had focused all his security effort outside the building. If so, that would be pure creamy éclair for the sleuthing siblings.

To avoid drawing attention to their presence, they didn't switch on any lights, but of course Twinks had produced from her reticule a small torch whose narrow beam guided them on their way towards the centre of the house. Once again his sister's sense of direction had Blotto agape with admiration for her.

One corridor led to another and it was a while before they found their way barred by a door. Twinks put a finger to her lips to anticipate any comment from her brother, then knelt down on the floor to peer through the keyhole into the space beyond. Having gained the information she required, she gestured to

Blotto to reverse along the corridor until they were safely out of hearing range from the room ahead.

'It's a spoffing great dining hall,' Twinks whispered. 'All lit up, and two men sitting drinking at one end of a long table. I'll lay a guinea to a groat that they're Gerhardt Sachs and Wellborough Choat.'

'Then let's shift like a pair of cheetahs in spikes and confront the stenchers!'

'No. Let's check out the lie of the land first.' Twinks could see the disappointment in her brother's face. Blotto was a spur-of-the-moment kind of a boddo; he thought planning things usually spoiled the fun. 'I saw through the keyhole,' she went on, 'that there's a kind of first-floor gallery running round the room. If we can find our way up there, we're rolling on camomile lawns. We can check up on what those bad tomatoes down there are up to.'

Reluctantly, Blotto acceded to his sister's wishes, and with the unfailing accuracy of a homing pigeon, Twinks led the way up some stairs to a small door which opened out on to the gallery she had described.

The room in which they found themselves was very large, rising up to the full height of the house. The ceiling was a high glass dome. In more clement weather glass panels on this could be opened by a system of pulleys which were attached to cleats on the gallery walls. Down below was a large dining hall, heated by two massive open fires on either side. Over the high mantelpieces of each was fixed a ceremonial display of weapons—swords, daggers, pikes—splaying out from behind a shield bearing the design of three crimson feathers.

Twinks led her brother along the gallery to the perfect vantage point, above the unoccupied end of the long table, with a good view of the two men hunched together over a brandy bottle. The sheepskin jacket he wore and the leather pilot's cap and gloves laid on the table beside him suggested that the stockier of the villains was Gerhardt Sachs. By a process of elimination the other one must be Wellborough Choat. He was tall and angular, with the features of a disdainful weasel and the look of a man who'd spent his childhood tearing the wings off robins.

'Shall we edge round the gallery and jump down on them like a couple of synchronized sacks of bricks?' suggested Blotto in a low whisper.

Twinks put a finger to her lips. 'No, let's find out what we can from up here first.'

'But we've got a dead dormouse's chance of finding out anything from up here.'

'Don't you believe it, Blotters. I happen to have a very powerful set of binoculars in my reticule.' And she reached into the aforesaid receptacle to produce the delicate silver instrument. She raised it to her azure eyes and focused on the hands of Gerhardt Sachs.

'Well, this is as easy as a barmaid's virtue,' she whispered.

'What do you mean, old pineapple?'

'I can read the letters tattooed on his middle finger from here.' She memorized the sequence: 'EOSN'.

'What about the other chap?'

Twinks shifted the beam of the binoculars to the hands of Wellborough Choat. 'Stencher's still wearing gloves,' she complained.

'Pity we can't hear what the slimers are saying,' observed Blotto.

'Oh, but we can. I have the perfect device to help us do that.'

'In your reticule?'

'Of course.' Twinks produced a small instrument with a long funnel-shaped tube attached to a black box with dials on it. 'It's a kind of electric long-range ear trumpet. You focus it like a light-beam and it magnifies the sound.'

She pointed the wide end towards the two men, set the other to her ear and, after a little judicious twiddling, listened intently. Then she grinned at her brother. 'Definitely on the right track, Blotto. They're talking about the League of the Crimson Hand. And the next outrage being planned by the Crimson Thumb.'

'Have they said what it is?'

'No. But it's going to be the biggest crime they've ever committed.'

'The stenchers! So we are going to have to confront them, aren't we?' asked Blotto, unable to suppress his excitement at the possible fray ahead.

'Possibly. Just rein in the roans for a moment while I have a little cogitette.'

As ever, respectful of his sister's superior brain power, Blotto was patiently silent. After a moment, Twinks announced her plan. 'Assuming, as seems to be the case, that all the guards are on the outside, I think we should lock the main doors of the house. Then it'll just be two against two—make the odds a bit more even, what?'

'Uneven,' Blotto corrected her proudly. 'Any two people in the world against you and me are getting the wrong end of the sink-plunger, aren't they, Twinks?'

She smiled fondly at her brother. 'What larks!' she whispered. 'Larksissimo!'

'Shall I go and lock the doors?'

'No, I'll do it.' She didn't need to remind him of her superior sense of direction. Blotto nodded acquiescence. 'And don't fire the starting pistol till I'm back and in my blocks—tickey-tockey?'

'Tickey-tockey, Twinks.'

After she'd disappeared through the gallery door, though, Blotto began to feel the stirrings of rebellion. He'd never question, when it came to brainwork, that his sister was a few millennia ahead of him, but on the physical stuff he always won the rosette. And, after all, what they were facing wasn't a big job. Just capturing the two bad tomatoes on the floor below. Blotto would have the advantage of surprise and, given the way they were putting away the brandy, he didn't think his opponents would be at their sharpest. It'd save time, too. He imagined the smile of pride on Twinks's face when she returned to the gallery to find that the next stage of their task had been completed.

For some time he had been eyeing the ropes designed to open and close the panels of the room's glass dome, and calculating angles. Though his mathematical skills at Eton had been on a par with all of his other academic achievements ('Lyminster Minor,' one school report had read, 'has yet to provide evidence that he possesses a brain'), when it came to practical problems he could show remarkable acuity.

His computations complete, Blotto unwound the double ropes he had selected from their cleat and gave them few exploratory tugs to see that they were safely secured above. Then, assessing the requisite lengths for his purposes, he tied the parallel ropes together at two points. He climbed on to the rail of the gallery. Placing his right foot in the lower loop he'd created, and clasping his left hand firmly above the higher knot, he launched himself out into the space below.

He'd got the distances just perfect. His body swung in an arc across the room, two feet above the floor at the lowest point of his trajectory. As he had anticipated, his first point of contact was the wall above the mantelpiece of the fire opposite. From the display of weapons there, he extracted a heavy broadsword before kicking off on a new course which sent him powering like a wrecking-ball towards the two men at the end of the table.

Gerhardt Sachs and Wellborough Choat looked up in amazement at the human missile hurtling towards them. As he closed in, Blotto opened his legs to the perfect angle, so that each of the villains received a sole of (rather damp) patent leather dress shoe full in the face.

The impact was such that both men were sent flying backwards, taking their chairs with them. Gerhardt Sachs lay still, winded or perhaps unconscious, while Wellborough Choat stumbled confusedly to his feet. By the time he was upright, he saw that Blotto had detached himself from the ropes and was standing on the table, wielding the large broadsword which had probably been captured by the Welsh in battle with some Norman Marcher Baron.

'Give yourself up!' commanded Blotto. 'Take off your gloves, Wellborough Choat, and show me what you have tattooed on your index finger!'

Feigning compliance, the tall man fumbled as if removing his gloves, but in fact produced a gun—a double-action Frimmelstopf Derringer. He pointed it up towards his adversary's chest and pulled the trigger.

Blotto moved sideways quickly enough to evade the bullet, though he felt it take a chunk of black herringbone wool out of his tailcoat. But Wellborough Choat was already lining up the second shot.

Remembering his many hours cricket training in the nets, Blotto dropped to one knee and executed the perfect Sweep to Leg. He kept his broadsword blade angled downwards to deflect his primary target, the bullet from the double-action Frimmelstopf Derringer, which ricocheted satisfyingly to bury itself into the table. In the same movement, he straightened the blade so that the flat of it caught Wellborough Choat full on the shoulder and sent him flying to the floor. The villain ended up propped against the wainscot, battered and dazed.

'I thought I told you to wait for me, me old trombone.' Blotto turned at the sound of his sister's dry voice behind him.

She was walking up the hall, not looking as pleased with him as was her custom.

'I just thought—'

'How many times, Blotto, have I told you that thinking isn't your cut of the joint? I'm the whale of whales when it comes to thinking.'

'Yes, but fair biddles, Twinks me old tea tray. I'm a whale on the violent stuff. And there's no thinking involved.'

'Blotto, are you advocating the practice of mindless violence?'

'Well, I, er, um...'

'Anyway, no time to fritter. I'm going to rescue Laetitia Melmont. You check what's tattooed on this stencher.'

'Good ticket, Twinks. Do you have a notebook in your reticule?'

'What for?'

'To write down the new letters with the other ones.'

'I haven't written anything down, Blotto. That might be a security risk if my reticule fell into the wrong hands. I've memorized the other letters.'

'Ah,' said Blotto, once again awe-struck by his sister's superior mental capacity 'You must have a spoffing set of filing cabinets in that little brainbox of yours, Twinks.'

'Oh, what guff!'

'Anyway, you want me to do the same? Memorize the letters.'

'Exactly.'

Her brother nodded. 'Order received and understood, as your swain Jerome Handsomely would put it.'

Twinks went off to rescue Laetitia Melmont. Blotto's task was easy. Wellborough Choat was still far too concussed to resist having his index finger checked.

Blotto read the letters: 'WELT'. Odd, what on earth can that mean? he asked himself. Part of a shoe, isn't it? He said the word to himself three or four times, hoping that would imprint the sequence indelibly on his memory. He would have repeated it a few more times, just to be sure, had not his sister come rushing back into the dining hall with a cry of 'Laetitia's not there!'

She took in the scene around her and then demanded, 'Just a minute. What's happened to the other bad tomato?'

Blotto looked with surprise at the spot where Gerhardt Sachs had ended up in a crumpled heap. There was no sign of him. What's more, his sheepskin jacket, leather cap and gloves had disappeared from the table. The villain must have slipped away while he had been concentrating on Wellborough Choat.

Blotto and Twinks looked at each other, realization as usual dawning rather quicker on her face than his. 'He must have got Laetitia!' she shouted.

Even as they rushed to the door, through chinks in the curtain came light from the reilluminated airstrip. At the same time they heard the ominous sound of a Frimmelstopf Fliegflügel being started up.

'Oh, broken biscuits!' said Blotto.

They turned at a new sound: the front doors of the dining hall being crashed open. The uniformed guards had managed to get inside the house.

Blotto and Twinks found themselves facing twenty uniformed men with rifles at the ready.

'Larksissimo!' murmured Twinks.

'Hoopee-doopee!' murmured Blotto.

Chapter Twenty-one

Back to Croydon Aerodrome

Blotto managed to defeat the twenty uniformed men with rifles who were guarding Llanystwyth House—usual thing, he'd have preferred to have his cricket bat with him, but he wasn't so dusty with his bare hands—and then escorted his sister through to the garages at the back. There he commandeered a Frimmelstopf roadster and they set off along the narrow lanes of Wales in the direction of Croydon Aerodrome.

The first few miles were a bit scary, because some of the guards came after them on motor bicycles, but Blotto's expert driving managed to shake them off—literally, in most cases. A whole lot of motor bicycle and guard debris was found in the valleys of the Black Mountains the following morning.

Blotto and Twinks didn't have much opportunity to talk during the pursuit, but they relaxed when it was clear nobody else was following them. The roads were empty as they descended into the little town of Cwmgwynt. Their immediate troubles were, it seemed, over.

At that moment, however, the Frimmelstopf roadster shuddered to a halt in the town centre, and no amount of efforts on the self-starter from Blotto suggested that its engine would ever start again.

'Murdy Continental workmanship!' he said eventually, giving the car's wheel housing a kick of pure frustration.

'These tin toys are not a patch on the Lagonda. Oh, how I wish I had that little breathsapper with me at this moment!'

'Well, you don't,' said Twinks, practical as ever. 'So it's no use chewing over old cud. We need to shift our shimmies out of this place before the League of the Crimson Hand get the bizz-buzz on what we've done and widen the search for us.'

'That's easy enough to say, Twinks me old brass door-knocker, but *how* are we going to get out of this place?'

They looked around. The first brushstrokes of dawn had been laid over the darkness of the night, and they could see that the town of Cwmgwynt was small and depressed, presumably by being in Wales. The cottages seemed to cling together for comfort. There was an uninviting hotel called The Golden Sheep, some unwelcoming shops and an unamused chapel. Because of the time—by now about half past six in the morning—everything was shut. The only person on the streets was a dispirited-looking milkman, too caught up in his own thoughts even to notice the unusual sight in Cwmgwynt of a couple dressed for dinner at the Savoy.

'Hotels usually either have their own hire cars or know where they can be procured,' Twinks announced, stepping determinedly towards The Golden Sheep.

The front door was locked, but she had no hesitation in ringing the Night Bell. Equally she had no hesitation in telling the sleepy porter who opened up for them that she needed him to organize a car 'and put a jumping cracker under it!' Nor did hesitation feature in her ordering the porter to wake up the local garage owner and someone to drive them in the hire car to Croydon Aerodrome. Twinks was, basically, born to rule, and, given that she was so aristocratic and beautiful, her inferiors everywhere gloried in being bossed around by her.

Because of the chauffeur in front, during the long, tedious journey from Cwmgwynt, Blotto and Twinks did not dare to speak of the case which they were investigating. Blotto suggested playing some of the guessing games they had played on journeys as children, but after his sister had won the first thirty-four rounds the idea seemed to pall. No opportunities for him to crow, 'So snubbins to you, Twinks!'

For the rest of the journey silence hung between them. It was a silence which comprised boredom and, neither could deny, a strong anxiety. Though they were making headway in their investigation of the League of the Crimson Hand, Laetitia Melmont had been abducted once again and they were still far from being the winners of the contest.

It was early evening by the time they reached Croydon Aerodrome. While Blotto paid off the driver—and decided that buying a new car might have been cheaper—Twinks hurried into the booking hall and again gave a message for Jerome Handsomely. This time, though, the pilot wasn't on the premises.

Nor, to the deep chagrin of Blotto, was his Lagonda. The space where they had last seen it was empty. His face took on the expression of a mother sheep who had just seen her ewe-lamb served up with mint sauce and redcurrant jelly. 'Toad-in-the-hole!' he murmured savagely. 'Now we know exactly what kind of stenching rotten tomatoes we are up against.'

The driver who had been commandeered in Cwmgwynt would not have dared to refuse the command to drive Blotto and Twinks back to Tawcester Towers. But in fact it suited him quite well. Going via the Lyminster seat would not involve much of a detour on his route back to Wales. And he was being paid by the mile.

Still having a potential eavesdropper in the driving seat, the aristocratic sleuths were again prevented from discussing their investigation. Nothing Twinks did by the way of smiles and reassurances could lift the pall of despair that had settled on her brother. 'We'll find the Lagonda,' she kept insisting. 'We'll find it.'

But Blotto's spirits remained as low as a carpet's underfelt. At one point, when they were driving through Oxford, he let out a groan so deep that his sister feared for his health.

'What is it, Blotto me old gumdrop?'

'I've just realized. Not only have the stenchers taken the Lag, but they've got its contents too…including my cricket bat!'

Twinks did not underestimate the seriousness of the situation. There were three things that Blotto held dear in life, three things for which his love exceeded anything he could feel for a mere woman—his hunter Mephistopheles, his Lagonda and his cricket bat. Now of the three he only had Mephistopheles. If her brother was not to waste away from a broken heart, the Lagonda and the cricket bat must be reclaimed as quickly as possible. The sooner they could confront the Crimson Thumb, the better.

It was not until the early hours, when their driver, smiling from a well-filled wallet, deposited them in front of the main doors of Tawcester Towers, that Twinks was finally able to pose the question she had been longing to since they had left Llanystwyth House. 'So, Blotto me old battledore, tell me,' she said as they entered their ancestral home, 'what were the letters?'

Her brother looked puzzled. 'Letters?'

'The letters which will give us the clue to the whereabouts of the Crimson Thumb. The letters which you read from the index finger of Wellborough Choat and then memorized.'

His brow cleared. 'Oh, those letters.'

'Well, what are they?'

There was a silence while Blotto raked through the empty prairies of his brain. Then he said, 'Um…'

'What?'
Another 'Um...'
'What are they, Blotto?'
'Twinks, me old sideboard...'
'Yes?'
'I'm afraid I've forgotten them.'

Chapter Twenty-two

A Devilish Puzzle

When they awoke the next morning, Blotto and Twinks took great pleasure in putting on clothes other than the evening wear which they'd had on since their abortive attempt to dine at the Savoy Grill. But when they went downstairs to breakfast, they found Tawcester Towers virtually in mourning. Sloggo, the wife of Loofah (a.k.a. the Duke of Tawcester), had recently been brought to bed of a child. Which would have been very exciting and a cause for great celebration, but for the fact that she had produced yet another girl. The Tawcester ducal line had once again failed to be extended into another generation. Its continuity still rested on the unreliable shoulders of Blotto. The Dowager Duchess was in a state of apoplectic fury.

Said fury was not diminished by the discovery that her son—it would never occur to her to blame her daughter for such shortcomings—had allowed Laetitia Melmont to be abducted from under his protection, not once but twice. 'This is in danger of becoming a habit with you, Blotto,' she fulminated. 'You did the same thing with that other wretched girl, the ex-King of Mitteleuropia's daughter Ethelinda.'

'Well, it wasn't exactly the same,' Blotto protested.

But his counter-arguments were, as ever, swept away like tissue paper in a tornado. 'What matters is, Blotto, not the precise similarities between the two instances, but the fact that you are once again getting yourself in a position where the family honour can only be maintained by your rescuing a young woman.'

'Don't worry, I will rescue her.'

'Well, I hope you do. I hope also, Blotto, that you are fully aware of the obligation your rescuing Laetitia Melmont will put you under.'

'Er...not quite on the same page as you, Mater...?'

'Any man who rescues an abducted woman will, almost of necessity, have had to spend a certain amount of time alone with that woman.'

'Ye-es,' Blotto agreed cautiously. 'But where's the chock in the cogwheel there?'

'The view of Society,' his mother pontificated heavily, 'is that when a young man and a young woman spend time alone together, they are automatically putting themselves under an obligation.'

'To do what?' asked Blotto wretchedly, all too sure that he knew the forthcoming answer.

It came. 'They have to get married,' the Dowager Duchess pronounced. 'And in the case of Laetitia Melmont, there are of course other pressing reasons why you two should tie the knot.'

'What are they?' came the feeble response.

'Her mother, the Dowager Duchess of Melmont, was very enthusiastic about the match. Since Pansy is now dead, that enthusiasm has effectively become a dying wish. And it is thought impolite to deny the dying wishes of members of the aristocracy—particularly when they have been murdered.'

If he had dared, Blotto would have groaned audibly. As it was, he contented himself with a silent groan.

'Furthermore,' his mother continued, 'Laetitia Melmont is Catholic. And Catholics are even less tolerant than normal people of unchaperoned young persons of different genders being alone together. They have some very odd ideas when it comes to...certain unpalatable duties.' This was the closest the Dowager Duchess ever got to the mention of sex, something she had tolerated with the late Duke three times (to produce an heir, a spare and a daughter), and to which she had subsequently closed her mind (amongst other things).

'No, I'm afraid there is no way around it, Blotto. If you fail to rescue Laetitia Melmont, you will have besmirched the honour of the Tawcesters! If you succeed in rescuing her, you will be obliged to marry her.'

What a gluepot, thought Blotto miserably, what a spoffingly fumacious gluepot!

Normally, after a sand-blasting from the Dowager Duchess, he would go to Twinks's boudoir, where his sister was unfailingly ready to provide reassurance and cheeriness. But that particular day she reacted to him almost as frostily as his mother had.

'Come on, Twinks me old carrot cake, what's put lumps in your custard? Tell me what I've done wrong.'

'If you don't know, then you're stupider than I thought you were.'

Blotto was shocked. He'd heard his sister talk that way to some of her amorous swains, which had been fair enough, but she'd never before used language like that to him. It was a measure of how deeply he had upset her. And he hadn't a clue why. What could he have done that would so change her usually tolerant attitude to him?

'Sorry, not on the same page,' he said feebly.

Twinks looked at him and her expression softened. She found it almost impossible to be cross with her brother for long. 'Blotto, what you have done wrong is to fail to remember the letters tattooed on Wellborough Choat's index finger.'

'Ah, with you, me old greengage. Sorry about that. Bit of a candle-snuffer, isn't it?'

'There are twenty-six letters in the alphabet. I'm only asking you to remember four of them.'

'Good ticket. You make it sound easy.' His brows furrowed as he sifted through the contents of his brain. The exercise did not take long. 'Sorry, Twinks. It's a dead dormouse, I'm afraid. Nobody at home in the memory department.'

'Maybe you could remember *some* of the letters?'

He considered this suggestion for a moment, then shook his head. 'Sorry, could be any of the twenty-six.'

Twinks sighed and turned to the large sheet of paper on her dressing table. Taking a silver propelling pencil out of her reticule, she wrote down three groups of four letters each. They read: GGEC LLRA EOSN.

'What are those?' asked Blotto.

Patiently his sister reminded him, 'These are the letters we found tattooed on the fingers of Will Tyler, Davy ap Dafydd and Gerhardt Sachs.'

'Ah, tickey-tockey, with you. Back on the same page.'

'They represent three-quarters of the information which would take us to the lair of the Crimson Thumb.'

'So how do they do that?'

'Anagram.'

'Who's she?' asked Blotto.

'No, not "Anna Gram". "Anagram".'

'And what's that when it's got its clothes on?'

'An anagram is a word made up from the letters of another word or words.'

'Er?'

'Like, for instance, "star" is an anagram of "rats"—or indeed "tars" or "tsar".'

'Is it, by strawberries?' asked Blotto, still befuddled.

'Look, here's another example. The third sequence of letters here—"EOSN", the one that was tattooed on Gerhardt Sachs's hand—is an anagram of "nose".'

'Ah.' Enlightenment dawned in Blotto's honest features. 'So if we can find his nose, then we can find the rest of the Crimson Thumb.'

'That is undeniably true, Blotto, but it wasn't the point I was trying to put across.'

'Oh.' He looked deflated. 'So can you make one of these anaconda things—?'

'Anagram.'

'Yes, that. Can you make one out of the letters you've got there?'

Twinks glanced down at the letters she had written down. GGEC LLRA EOSN. After a couple of seconds she announced, '"CALL EGG-NOSER". "CLARE'S GONE L.G.". Or "ROG CAGES NELL".'

Blotto was aghast with admiration. 'How do you do that, Twinks?'

'I do a lot of crosswords,' she replied dismissively.

'But it's spoffulatingly clever.' He grinned with triumph. 'And you've solved the case for us. All we have to do now is find these people—Clare, Rog, Nell and whoever the "egg-noser" is and we—'

'Blotto,' his sister interposed gently, 'these anagrams are meaningless. We'll only get the anagram we want when we've got the four other letters, the ones that were tattooed on Wellborough Choat's index finger.'

'Oh, biscuits!' said Blotto. 'We're back to that, are we?'

'Still no recollection of what you saw?'

Blotto's face was so scrunched up with the effort of remembering that, for a moment, he almost ceased to look handsome. Eventually he announced, 'No, sorry, it's gone.'

'Hm. Well, maybe we'll have to use scientific methods to dig it out.' And Twinks reached into her reticule.

Her brother was alarmed. 'What're you up to, old pine-apple? Are you going to drill holes in my brainbox?'

'No, nothing so dramatic. I'll just use this.' And from the reticule she produced a piece of ribbon with what looked like a pendant on the end.

'What the strawberries is that?' asked Blotto.

'It is something I have sometimes used for mesmerism.'

'Er?'

'Hypnotism.'

'Er?'

'I will use it to put you into a trance.'

'Oh?'

Twinks raised her hand and let the pendant swing from side to side in front of her brother's puzzled blue eyes. 'You are going to sleep,' she intoned.

'No, I'm not. It's nowhere near bedtime and I—' Blotto's chin slumped forward on to his chest.

'You are in a deep sleep now,' Twinks intoned, 'and you will stay in that sleep until I wake you by snapping my fingers. Now, Blotto, I want you to go back in time.' Her brother started crying like a baby. 'No, not that far back. I want you to go back to the moment in the early hours of yesterday morning, when you looked at Wellborough Choat's hand in Llanystwyth House...Are you there yet? Are you there yet?'

Blotto nodded. Suppressing her excitement, Twinks continued in the same level, spell-binding tone. 'What do you see tattooed on Wellborough Choat's index finger?'

After a long silence, Blotto announced: 'Shoe.'

'"Shoe"!' Twinks turned gleefully to the dressing table and added the four letters to the existing twelve. Then she tried producing anagrams. She very quickly got 'CHEESE ROLL GAG, SON', which possibly sounded like an order from an oikish person in a café, but which didn't seem to have much relevance to the League of the Crimson Hand. Nor was 'L.E.C. EGGS ARE ON HOLS' much more helpful. In fact, nothing she came up with seemed to work.

Cast down, she turned back to her entranced brother. 'Blotto, are you sure it was "shoe"?'

'To do with shoe,' came the inert reply.

'To do with "shoe"? A four-letter word to do with shoe. Sole!' Twinks cried gleefully.

She returned to her propelling pencil and paper. At lightning speed she wrote down 'ALL GREEN COGS LOSE' and 'LARGE LEG COOLNESS'. But, though she felt some satisfaction in working them out, once again she couldn't see how either solution was about to help their investigation.

'Other words to do with shoe...?' Twinks had a go adding 'lace' to her anagram. The results—CLEAN CLOG REGALES and CLEGG'S REAL ALE CON—may have been intellectually pleasing, but didn't lead to any destination.

Starting to feel a bit desperate by now, she tried adding 'heel', which produced the nugatory anagram 'GALES LEECH LONGER'. With the same letters she got momentarily excited that she'd identified the Crimson Thumb as 'NOEL CRAGSHELL-GEE', but then remembered Will Tyler had confirmed that the letters would lead to his headquarters rather than the man himself.

Furious with her lack of progress, Twinks looked down at her own dainty slipper as a visual aid and tried to think of a four-letter part of it she hadn't already used. Finding nothing, her scrutiny moved to her brother's black brogues. And there she saw it. Joining the upper to the sole was a...'welt'.

'GGEC LLRA EOSN WELT'. So obvious.

Instantly she wrote the solution down. Then snapping her fingers to wake her bemused brother, she told him she knew where the headquarters of the Crimson Thumb was.

'Where?' asked Blotto blearily.

'Glenglower Castle,' announced a triumphant Twinks.

Chapter Twenty-three

Preparing for a Confrontation

Twinks kept a comprehensive research library at the back of one of the wardrobes in her boudoir, and it was a matter of moments for her to produce from it a gazetteer, an atlas and a copy of *Burke's Peerage*.

Only a few more moments were required for her to locate Glenglower Castle. It was in Argyllshire, on the Firth of Lorne, just a little south of Oban. And the *Peerage* informed her that the castle was the ancestral seat of the Earls of McCluggan.

A further rummage in her wardrobe produced an illustrated volume called *The Ancient Castles of Scotland (With Engravings on Steel)*. She quickly flicked through to the relevant illustration and turned over the page of translucent paper which protected it. Revealed was a forbidding stone structure with many turrets, set on a rocky outcrop on the edge of what could have been the sea or perhaps a large loch.

Twinks grew pensive. 'I don't like the look of this.'

'The look of what?' asked Blotto.

'Glenglower Castle is owned by an aristocrat...well, only a Scottish one, true, but still a sort of aristocrat...'

'And...?'

'And the League of the Crimson Hand is an organization dedicated to the destruction of the aristocracy...'

'Ye-es.'

'But their headquarters is in Glenglower Castle.'

'Sorry, not on the same page, Twinks me old bicycle pump.'

She explained: 'Look, an aristocrat is not going to support an organization whose sole purpose is the coffination of the entire aristocracy. Not even a Scottish one.'

'Take your point.'

'So I'm beginning to wonder whether the owner of Glenglower Castle is in fact being held there against his will.'

'Well, if so, he must've been held there a spoffing long time. I mean, it would have taken a while to get all those boddos' hands tattooed. They wouldn't do that if Glenglower Castle was just a temporary address, would they?'

'No.'

'Anyway, who is the owner of Glenglower Castle?' Twinks once again consulted *Burke's Peerage*. 'He's called The McCluggan of McCluggan.'

'Do we know anything about the poor old thimble?'

'I've never heard the name before. I wonder if he often attends the House of Lords...?'

'Why?'

'Because, if he does, Loofah might have met him, mightn't he?'

'Good ticket, Twinks.' A shadow crossed Blotto's brow. 'But then again, it's pretty unlikely. I mean, when did Loofah last attend the House of Lords? Except of course for last year's Christmas lunch.'

Twinks nodded, acknowledging the lapse in her thinking. In common with many other peers, their brother the Duke of

Tawcester had absolutely no interest in politics. So long as no legislation was brought in to diminish his wealth and power, he was quite content for the country to be run by people of the oikish classes in the House of Commons.

'Do you know anyone else in the Lords who we could ask about The McCluggan of McCluggan?' asked Blotto.

Of course she did. Twinks had contacts everywhere. In most cases they were men who had asked her to marry them and been brushed off with the firm delicacy of a cat-lover stroking a kitten. In the current necessity the right person to ask was the Marquis of Godalming. Twinks went down to Tawcester Towers' one telephone in the hall, and asked the operator to connect her with the Marquis's number.

'Chinless,' she said when she got through, 'it's Twinks.'

'Twinks! How dashed wonderful to hear your voice. My feelings haven't changed for you, you know. You have only to say the word and I'll be at your side in as long as it takes. I'll abandon Godalming Towers, leave the Marchioness and the eight children. I'll—'

'Chinless,' said Twinks purposefully, 'I'm not ringing you about anything like that.'

'Oh.' Disappointment suffused the monosyllable.

'I am ringing because I happen to know that you attend the House of Lords with admirable frequency...'

'So would anyone who was married to the Marchioness and had eight children.'

'...and there's a Scottish peer, a laird, about whom I require some information.'

'Anything you want, Twinks,' said the Marquis of Godalming miserably. 'You know I'll do absolutely anything for you. I wish it could be—'

'Chinless,' she pressed on, 'the name of the peer in question is The McCluggan of McCluggan. His seat is Glenglower Castle in Argyllshire and I am anxious to get any information about him. Do you know the boddo, Chinless?'

'Used to.'

'Why do you say "used to"?'

'Because it's years since the old thimble has actually put in an appearance in the House of Lords.'

'Oh?'

'Used to be one of the more regular attendees. Turned up on the benches as often as I did. Then suddenly—no sign of him.'

'Did you discover any reason for his non-attendance?'

'Who knows? I mean, I wasn't close to the blighter. Might meet up for the odd scotch and soda in the bar, bemoan the way the Socialists were trying to do away with our God-given privileges, that sort of thing.'

'Ah,' said Twinks, fully aware of the significance of his words. 'But you don't know anything else about him?'

'Heard from another Scottish peer that The McCluggan'd gone to ground in...wherever it is he lives.'

'Glenglower Castle.'

'That's the one. Anyway, apparently the blighter's turned reclusive. Not been seen out anywhere—even at the Highland Games, which, as the local laird, he used never to miss. Said to be quite a connoisseur of tossing the caper.'

'Caber, I think.'

'Whatever you say, Twinks.'

'But had he ever struck you as reclusive before, Chinless?'

'No, life and soul of the party, I'd have said. Certainly used to wake up the old snorers in the H. of L.'

'Hm...Well, thank you for telling me all that, Chinless. I must—'

'Are you sure there's no chance for me? As I say, I'd abandon everything if you only...'

Twinks allowed him a small ration of abject adoration before the gracious, but inevitable, brush-off. She replaced the receiver and looked at Blotto, who had been hanging around, trying to piece together the whole conversation from what he'd heard Twinks say.

'So what's the bizz-buzz?' he asked.

His sister looked serious as she replied, 'I think the number of reasons for our solving this case has suddenly increased.'

'Oh?'

'We first got into it to free Corky Froggett by working out who really killed the Dowager Duchess of Melmont. Then the abduction of Laetitia Melmont gave us a second reason. Now I reckon we could also be investigating the incarceration—or possibly even murder—of The McCluggan of McCluggan.'

'Broken biscuits,' said Blotto. Things were that serious.

He wandered disconsolately down to the Tawcester Towers garages. Normally the place gave him quite a buzz. Almost as much as driving it, he loved just being with his Lagonda. And there was nothing he liked better than discussing its superiority to all other marques with Corky Froggett.

But now the chauffeur was languishing in jail, and Blotto had no idea where the Lagonda was. Though normally the cheeriest of souls, he did have difficulty in not being devastated by these two hammer-blows.

But there was the matter of suitable transport for him and Twinks to Glenglower Castle. It wasn't that the Tawcester Towers garages lacked for cars. There were some Rolls-Royces, the odd Hispano-Suiza, and a few perfectly adequate Bentleys.

But none of them had the appeal for Blotto of the Lagonda. Driving one of the others was always going to be second best— or, in Blotto's jaded view, about a millionth best. When he was driving the Lagonda, it was hard to tell where car stopped and man started. With any other vehicle the distinction between car and man was painfully marked.

Miserably Blotto went to ask his sister's advice. He was very relieved by Twinks's recommendation that they should not go by car. Instead they should take the train to Oban and a small branch line to McCluggan Halt, the nearest station to Glenglower Castle.

Before they departed for the north, Twinks was very keen to contact Jerome Handsomely. She left a message for him at Croydon Aerodrome, but it was a few hours before he telephoned back. At that time Twinks was out riding, so the Tawcester Towers butler Grimshaw summoned Blotto to take the call.

'Hello, Jerome,' he said. 'What's up? Uncage the ferrets, me old greengage.'

'Had a message from the lovely Twinks, me old propeller-winder. Apparently she needs help, and I'm absolutely snuffled-up to hear that. You know I'd readily lay down my life for—'

Blotto, who'd already heard quite enough such assertions, interrupted. 'There've been developments in our ongoing battle with those stenchers, the League of the Crimson Hand.'

Quickly he filled in what had happened at Llanystwyth House after he and Twinks had parachuted out of Jerome Handsomely's plane. He also described how they had found the address of the League's headquarters. 'So we'll be shifting up north as fast as a pair of cheetahs on spikes. I think Twinks wanted to ask you if you could help us out with a bit of aerial support.'

'Great dithering dragonflies, of course I will! I'll be with you as fast as a whizzbang's wake. Only wasp in the jam is that I'm not actually in Blighty at the moment.'

'Oh? Where are you?'

'Transcarpathia. Taken my crate here on a top-secret government mission. But don't worry, that can wait. I'll twang off the tarmac quicker than a doctor's bill and be with you zappity-ping.'

'How will you find us?'

'Well, I set my crate's homing sights on Glenglower Castle, don't I?'

'Yes, but how will we meet up when we're there? Twinks and I are taking the train. What happens if you fly over us while we're still in it?'

'Yes, that's a knuckle-cracker, isn't it?'

'Toad-in-the-hole!' A beatific smile made its way across Blotto's countenance. It was the smile that only appeared on those rare occasions when he had an idea. 'Tell you what, Jerome, we could have a kite.'

'What, fly your own crate, you mean?'

'No. A kite. Child's toy. You know, lots of string and all that rombooley...'

'Ah. Yes.' A silence. 'What good would that do?'

'Well, the kite'd be flying high above the train and you'd spot it from your plane and then you'd know where we are.'

'Ye-es.' Jerome Handsomely tried to keep as much scepticism as possible out of his voice. He'd noticed that Twinks had mastered the art of letting her brother down gently when he suggested something silly. So he tried to do the same. He would do anything to keep in Twinks's good books. Even to the extent—in fact preferably to the extent—of laying down his life for her.

Chapter Twenty-four

To the North!

Blotto quite liked travelling by train. Of course he didn't have that liberated feeling that suffused him when he drove the Lagonda, but there was something restful about steaming through the countryside at high speed.

They travelled light. Only three suitcases each. And in one of Blotto's he had put his second-best cricket bat. It would never have the same emotional resonance as the one which had been spirited away with his Lagonda, but it was better than nothing. The knowledge that it was readily accessible from one of his valises provided a source of comfort.

Both he and his sister had taken books with them for the long journey. Twinks was reading the complete works of Tolstoy in the original Russian, and Blotto was hoping to get through another page of *The Hand of Fu Manchu*. But both of them were too excited by the confrontation that lay ahead to concentrate fully on their books.

And then of course there was the business of keeping the kite flying out of the train window. Blotto was convinced if they didn't have it on show for the entire journey, there was a severe danger of Jerome Handsomely not being able to find them. And, though Twinks had at first tried to persuade him the kite wasn't necessary because the pilot knew their destination, after a time, as she so often did, she acceded to her brother's wishes. So they took it in turns to act as Kite Monitor—even to the point of attending different sittings for lunch in the buffet car.

Twinks had been in charge of the journey planning. Blotto readily admitted that he wasn't as good at practical arrangements as his sister and had let her get on with it. She had organized a First Class compartment to themselves from Euston station to Glasgow Central. To get to Glasgow Queen Street they crossed the city in a cab, giving Blotto an opportunity to get a close-up view of oikish people—and oikish Scottish people at that. It was not an experience which he found particularly rewarding, and he was relieved when they were once again in the safety of a First Class compartment on the train to Oban. They both abandoned their books and just drank in the beauties through which the West Highland Line passed.

Continuing to alternate as Kite Monitor, after a while they both stayed in the corridor because it offered a better view. They were passing through a lush medieval landscape of deep Scottish greens. They passed crags and forests and the occasional castle perched on a hill. They saw lochs and glimpses of the sea, on whose horizon squatted the misty outlines of distant islands. For a short while the splendour of the countryside took their minds off the seriousness of the mission on which they were bound.

It was at Oban that Twinks first detected something odd. The porter who took their luggage on his trolley and to whom she directed her inquiry as to where they should board the branch line to McCluggan Halt gave her a distinctly suspicious look. And the train to which he pointed them was very new-looking. As were the rails on which it ran. The branch line seemed to be a recent addition to the service.

There was only one coach behind the trim little steam engine.

And Blotto and Twinks were the only passengers who boarded it. So he didn't bother putting their luggage in the rack. He lined up the five suitcases and sat with his smaller valise between his legs.

As the train puffed slowly out of Oban station, Blotto put the kite out of the window and started feeding line out to it. When he reckoned it was flying high enough, he tied the end of the string to the arm of a seat. 'Easier in a train that doesn't have corridors, isn't it?'

Twinks agreed absently. She seemed preoccupied by the train in which they found themselves. 'Why's it all so new?' she murmured to her brother

'Don't know, but I think the whole set-up's quite beezer. Comfy, anyway.' He looked curiously round the carriage. 'I say, Twinks, it doesn't say anywhere that this is First Class, does it?'

'That's because it isn't.'

'What?'

'When I made the booking, I was told there were no different classes on this service. Everyone travels in the same compartments.'

'Everyone? What, you mean people like us and...oikish people too...?'

'Yes.'

'Well, I'll be snickered...That kind of Socialist thinking'll never catch on, will it?'

'One hopes not.'

Blotto shook his head in bewilderment. 'Not travelling First Class...I'm certainly seeing the world today, aren't I, Twinks?'

His sister agreed, but she still looked troubled.

'What's up, old banana skin? Come on, uncage the ferrets.'

'It's just that I'm worried that we may be stepping into a trap.'

'In what way?'

'Well, I thought travelling by train we'd be incognito. But I'm afraid by making the booking all I may have done is to alert our enemies to our arrival.'

'Sorry, not on the same page, old fruitbat.'

'Suppose this whole branch line—like Glenglower Castle itself—is owned by the League of the Crimson Hand?'

'But what the strawberries makes you think it might be?'

Twinks opened her mouth to reply, but she didn't need to. Her suspicion was confirmed visually, as the front door of the carriage opened.

And they were faced by Wellborough Choat, pointing at them a very purposeful-looking Accrington-Murphy shotgun.

Chapter Twenty-five

Peril on the Branch Line

The tall man's expression was even more rodent-like than it had looked at Llanystwyth House. In his eye glowed the satisfaction of a bird that had just cornered a worm on a stone floor.

'Rather over-curious, you two, aren't you?' he said. 'And getting a little too close for comfort, so far as the Crimson Thumb's concerned.'

'Shoot us, by all means, if you want to,' suggested Twinks, 'but that will only delay the assault on Glenglower Castle. I've informed Scotland Yard of what you're up to.'

Wellborough Choat's smile grew wider. 'Nice try, but I don't believe you. You haven't got any evidence that would get Scotland Yard interested in our affairs.'

'We know that Will Tyler murdered the Dowager Duchess of Melmont,' asserted Twinks.

But their adversary only shrugged. 'So...a disaffected servant turns on his employer. Wouldn't be the first time, and

I'm sure it won't be the last. You have nothing to link Will Tyler to the League of the Crimson Hand.'

'He had tattoos on his fingers.'

'Really? Well, maybe he'd once been a sailor.'

'I can assure you that Scotland Yard does know everything that has been happening. What's more—'

'And I can assure you that Scotland Yard knows nothing about what's been happening. There is an Assistant Commissioner there who is a member of the League of the Crimson Hand. He tells us everything. I was on the telephone to him only an hour ago, and he assured me that neither of you had made any contact with Scotland Yard.'

'You're lying.'

'No, I think you're lying.'

Twinks tried to come up with a suitable riposte, but couldn't, because of course Wellborough Choat was right. She was lying.

'Anyway, the pair of you have become rather a nuisance, and the Crimson Thumb doesn't like people who are a nuisance. They have a tendency to interfere with his plans.'

'Like his plan for the latest outrage? The crime that's going to be bigger than any that the League has perpetrated before?'

Wellborough Choat looked annoyed that Twinks knew so much and asked instinctively, 'How did you find out about that?'

'I overheard you discussing it with Gerhardt Sachs at Llanystwyth House.'

'Oh, did you? Well, even more reason that your investigations into our affairs should stop. And I regret to say that the end of your investigations will have to coincide with the end of your lives.' He gestured with his shotgun. 'Move down to the end of the carriage.'

Blotto rose to his feet with his hands behind his back and he and Twinks edged in the direction the shotgun had indicated. There was a door at the end, presumably to link through to the carriages behind. Except in this case there were no carriages behind.

The same thoughts were going through both their minds. Wellborough Choat would make them open the door. Then he would shoot them and they would fall back on to the unfrequented track, where their bodies would either be left as carrion for the scavengers of the Highlands or removed by members of the League of the Crimson Hand. Either way no trace of them would be left.

Blotto and Twinks exchanged looks. They had been through some tough times together, and always somehow managed to escape. But their current predicament was on a different scale of jeopardy.

'Open the door!' commanded Wellborough Choat, as anticipated. His smile grew thinner and more evil. 'Do you feel strongly about which one of you I should kill first?'

To the considerable surprise of Twinks, Blotto instantly replied, 'My sister.' She knew he had always been very chivalrous but, though she admired the chivalric principle of 'Ladies first', she felt this was one of those occasions when it shouldn't be applied too rigorously.

'Very well,' said their would-be killer. 'Milady—' he sneered the word—'if you would oblige me by standing in the doorway?'

Twinks did as she was told, hoping against hope that Blotto had something up his sleeve.

It wasn't actually up his sleeve. It was behind his back. As Wellborough Choat raised the shotgun to take a bead on Twinks, Blotto produced his second-best cricket bat, which he had earlier sneaked out of his valise, and leapt forward. Confused by the movement, Wellborough Choat's aim wavered for a second. Long enough for Blotto to take a mighty swing upwards which knocked the shotgun and sent its deadly spray of bullets into the carriage roof.

Suddenly the cricket bat was all over Choat, battering him from different angles, sending the weapon flying out of his hands, manoeuvring him towards the open door and the fast-moving track beneath. One final blow from the bat sent him flying backwards out of the train. He landed head first and, as his body on the forest-lined track dwindled into the distance, it show no signs of life.

'Glad "Pinko" Fripworth, my old cricket coach at Eton, didn't see that innings,' Blotto observed. 'Not the most stylish display of my life.'

'Never mind. It worked! Sometimes in life style has to give way to expediency.'

'Tickey-tockey, me old fruitbat. You never said a truer word.'

Blotto and Twinks exchanged looks and hugged each other.

'Well done, anyway,' she purred. 'You may be my brother, but you'll always be my hero as well.'

Blotto let out an embarrassed, self-deprecatory snort. 'Don't talk such toffee, Twinks. You make me feel like a Grade A poodle.' But he actually rather liked it when his sister said things like that. 'Come on, what's next on the hymn sheet?'

'Next thing we do is: we get off this train before it reaches its destination.'

'Oh? Why?'

'Because if Wellborough Choat was on it, I'd lay a guinea to a groat that the driver and anyone else on board is also a member of the League of the Crimson Hand. And the moment we get to McCluggan Halt we'll be grabbed and incarcerated as surely as The McCluggan of McCluggan himself.'

'So what do we do, Twinks?'

'We wait till the train begins to slow down and we get out of that door as quick as two ferrets in a rabbit warren.'

'What about our luggage?'

'Leave it. Only take essentials.'

Blotto looked at his second-best cricket bat. 'This is all I need. I've never rated this old willow very highly, but when nudge comes to knockout, it certainly fits the pigeon-hole.'

'Well, I've got all my essentials in my reticule,' said Twinks.

Even as she spoke, they felt the motion of the train change. It was definitely slowing down. Blotto and Twinks again exchanged looks. In both pairs of blue eyes the same excitement glowed. The siblings were never so happy as when they were on a hazardous mission together.

'Right, jump!' said Twinks.

'I'm taking the kite,' said Blotto. He unhitched it and managed to pass the end of the string from the window round the back of the carriage to keep control of it. 'Otherwise Jerome Handsomely will never find us.'

Twinks once again chose not to point out the uselessness of the kite as a location marker. Blotto so rarely had ideas that it didn't do to condemn them.

He jumped first, perhaps hoping to be able to break his sister's fall when she did. But of course the train's motion left him behind on the track. Twinks leapt into the void, and landed as neatly as a butterfly on a flower petal. Both of them scurried off into the woods at the side of the track.

The wind through the trees was strong and had a salty tang, suggesting that they were near the Firth of Lorne. And also near their destination. They couldn't progress far into the wood with the kite, because its string kept getting tangled in the branches. So Blotto tied it firmly to a tree trunk and found that the wind off the sea kept it aloft. The trees thinned out into a flat field near where he'd fixed the kite, but it wasn't the way they were going.

They followed the direction of the railway line and soon found themselves on the edge of the woods. Up ahead stood the reality whose image they had seen in *The Ancient Castles of Scotland (With Engravings on Steel)*.

In the dying light of the autumn afternoon Blotto and Twinks looked up at the forbidding walls of stone that encased Glenglower Castle, the lair of the Crimson Thumb.

Chapter Twenty-six

Glenglower Castle

The darkness was their friend. They could see light at the castle's main gate, and see it reflected on the rifles of the men who stood there on guard.

'Shall we make a full-frontal attack?' suggested Blotto, more confident of his second-best cricket bat than he had been before it had dealt with Wellborough Choat.

'No,' replied Twinks.

'Oh, but come on, me old biscuit barrel, we do have the advantage of surprise.'

"That's the last thing we have, Blotto. When the train we were on arrives at McCluggan Halt, the driver—not to mention the members of the League of the Crimson Hand who were lined up to be our reception committee—will find our luggage and pretty soon after find the body of Wellborough Choat on the line. We couldn't have advertised our arrival more if we'd announced it in the *Daily Clarion*'s Court Circular.'

'Oh. Yes, I read your semaphore. So how do we get in?'

'We don't go in the main entrance.'

'That sounds all tickey-tockey, but suppose there isn't another way in?'

'There is.'

'How the strawberries do you know that?'

'Because I not only looked at the picture of Glenglower Castle in *The Ancient Castles of Scotland (With Engravings on Steel)*, I also read the accompanying article. And there it said that there had always been a secret passageway leading into the place, down at the edge of the Firth of Lorne. It leads up from a natural cave which can only be accessed at low tide.'

'But it might be high tide now, Twinks me old trouser button.'

'It might, but it isn't.'

'How do you know?'

'I checked the tide tables for the Argyllshire coast before we left Tawcester Towers.'

'Toad-in-the-hole,' said Blotto, 'you think of everything. You know, when you die, Twinks, they should take your brainbox and put it in the British Museum.'

'Don't talk such guff. All I was doing was making proper preparations.'

'Yes, but why don't I ever think of doing things like that?'

There were some questions that Twinks's generous nature preferred to leave unanswered. 'Come on,' she said, 'let's get down to the seashore.'

The sky was clear and a thin moon let out just enough light for them to see where they were going. Twinks led the way. Not only had she found out about the secret entrance to Glenglower Castle, she had also memorized the map which had accompanied the article in *The Ancient Castles of Scotland (With Engravings on Steel)*.

As they had hoped, they didn't meet anyone on the way to the Firth's edge. Either the League of the Crimson Hand didn't know about the secret entrance, or they didn't think anyone else would know about it. In a matter of minutes Blotto and Twinks found themselves on the narrow strand between the sea and the base of the crag on which Glenglower Castle stood. Close up, the huge turreted structure looked more threatening than ever.

Twinks marched straight to the cave entrance, a low semicircle of darkness set into the solid rock. Once again she produced from her reticule the small torch which had lighted their way through Llanystwyth House. They had to crouch to get under the low archway, but inside the space opened up above them. The floor was still smooth sand, and the beam of the upturned torch showed the shape of a natural cathedral, whose walls glistened with seaweed.

At the far end of the space a flight of steps which had been carved out of the solid rock led up to a small door. The stairs were very slippery and as they mounted them Blotto and Twinks held hands, the torch pointing down at their precarious footholds. After a couple of stumbles they reached the top and Twinks focused the beam on the door that barred their way.

Its state of dilapidation suggested that the new owners of Glenglower Castle were unaware of the thing's existence. The wood at the bottom had rotted, one of the hinges had gone and the metalwork of its locks had rusted away to almost nothing. Pulling the hasp and padlock away from the spongy wood was a matter of moments. The door almost fell apart as they opened it, and Blotto and Twinks soon found themselves on a continuation of the carved steps. These were drier and offered a safer footing on the route up into the castle, though there was still a strong smell of the sea below.

The steps, over a hundred in all, continued straight in one long incline, at the end of which Blotto and Twinks's passage was barred by a rusted metal panel in the roof of the cave. Inspection with the torch showed an accumulation of cobwebs and fungoid growth which suggested the trapdoor hadn't been opened for some generations.

Blotto pushed up against it with one hand. There was no give at all in the metal. He put down his second-best cricket bat and tried pushing with both hands. Still nothing. 'It's stuck as tight as a milliner's corset,' he announced.

'Having come this far,' said Twinks, 'there is no way we're not going to get inside the castle.' She once again darted the beam of her torch around the sides of the square above them. 'Maybe if we scrape some of the guff that's gathered round the edges…?'

Her brother needed no further prompting. He reached up with his bare hands and dug away at the accretion of the ages, closing his mind to the precise nature of the noxious substances he was getting under his fingernails. He was about to announce that the mission was hopeless when his hand snagged on something hard.

More clearing around the protrusion revealed three aligned rusty rings, two affixed to the cave wall, the other to the trapdoor. Through them a rusty metal bar had been fixed, making an effective lock which could not be opened from the other side.

The rings and bar had been fused by rust, but two substantial whacks with Blotto's second-best cricket bat loosened them. A third blow to the end of the bar sent it flying out of the fixture and clattering down the rocky walls until it embedded itself in the soft sand beneath.

'Right. Let's have another pop at the partridge,' said Blotto. He planted his feet firmly on the top step, set both hands on the underside of the trapdoor and heaved upwards.

At first nothing seemed to be happening. Then there was a slight creaking noise and accumulated sand and other debris began to trickle from one side of the metal square. Blotto, realizing that that must be the side that opened, shifted his stance to apply maximum pressure there. He could feel sweat forming at his temples and down his back, he could feel his biceps straining against his shirt as finally, slowly, the trapdoor lifted.

No light appeared through the widening chink, which was good news. People need light and the lack of it suggested the space above them was unoccupied.

A couple more shoves and the three unhinged sides of the trapdoor were all free of their grooves. The only thing that prevented Blotto from opening it further was his own lack of height. But the metal square was moving quite freely now, so he got Twinks to climb on his shoulders and she pushed it back up into an upright position. As it passed the vertical, she let go, anticipating a huge crash as it fell to the ground, a huge crash that might well announce their arrival to every member of the League of the Crimson Hand inside Glenglower Castle.

But the trapdoor didn't crash down flat. Quickly meeting some obstruction, the sheet of metal rested safely against it.

From her brother's shoulders Twinks had no problem pulling herself up into the space above them. Then she reached down a hand to help Blotto up.

She had shielded the light of the torch by pressing the business end into her dress, but now cautiously brought it out to explore the room in which they had found themselves. It was very small, little more than a cupboard. In fact, as she moved the torch beam around she saw that it actually *was* a cupboard. The dust on the piles of what looked like old weapons, chains and manacles suggested that no one had opened its doors for a long time. Which perhaps explained the castle owners' ignorance of the sea entrance's existence.

Anticipating another lock to be broken, Blotto pushed gently against the cupboard door, but obligingly it gave and opened. The two of them stepped out into a narrow passage, again carved out of the solid rock. The end nearest to them had been blocked off by fallen rubble, but in the other direction there was a distant glimmer of light. Blotto and Twinks exchanged looks, both put their fingers to their lips and advanced towards it.

From what they could judge, the corridor along which they were progressing turned at right angles into the lit area. They could hear no sounds of human activity, but still kept their own noise to a minimum. At the turn, Twinks gave a quick look around the corner before signifying to Blotto that they were safe to continue.

The lighting in the new corridor came from gas lamps set high on the walls. On the opposite side were a row of heavily studded doors, whose square unglazed windows were thickly barred. No light came from the first one, into which Twinks directed her torch beam, but what she saw inside confirmed her suspicion that they had found the dungeons of Glenglower Castle. The slimy walls were pierced by no other windows, and the empty manacles hanging down from hooks symbolized the misery of those who had been incarcerated there. The only comforting fact was that the dungeon did not appear to have been used for a long time.

The second cell was more or less identical to the first, but from the opening in the door of the third light spilled. Switching off her torch, Twinks moved quietly forward to look inside.

Sitting alone at a table, she saw an elderly man with a magnificent greying ginger beard and eyebrows. He was wearing full Highland dress—a bonnet decorated with pheasant feathers, a short jacket and waistcoat with silver buttons, kilt, sporran and elaborately laced shoes over thick grey socks. Above the top of one sock protruded about two inches of his dagger, or *sgian dubh*.

Confident that they had been successful in at least the first part of their rescue plan, Twinks pushed open the door of the dungeon and pronounced in perfect Scots, '*Guid eenin!*'

The elderly man turned in surprise. But, like most of his gender, he was pleased to see Twinks.

'You,' she went on, 'must be The McCluggan of McCluggan.'

'I am that,' he admitted. 'And ye twae must be the younger son and daughter o' the Dowager Duchess of Tawcester.'

'We spotting well are!' said Blotto. 'And we have come to rescue you from the evil clutches of the League of the Crimson Hand and their stencher of a leader, the Crimson Thumb!'

The McCluggan of McCluggan smiled. 'I cannae thank ye enough,' he said, with something that sounded very much like relief.

Chapter Twenty-seven

Betrayed!

The McCluggan of McCluggan led the way out of his cell and towards the main body of the castle. The next two cells they passed were dark as pitch, but from the grating of the third a thin light emanated. A look through the aperture revealed Laetitia Melmont, sitting at a humble table reading a book (which they subsequently discovered to be *The Spiritual Exercises of St Ignatius*).

The keys to the cells, hanging from a hook on the wall opposite, were pointed out by the laird. 'How many times in mae miserable solitude I hae seen they keys and wished I could reach across and tak them tae achieve mae liberty,' he said.

'But in fact,' Twinks pointed out, 'the door to your cell was unlocked.'

The McCluggan of McCluggan raised his eyes to heaven. 'I ken weel. And I hae lang sin gi'en up the idea o' walking oot of it. The castle is aswarm with the League o' the Crimson Hand. Everich time I tried to escape—once I even got as far as the courtyard—I'd be recaptured and brought back tae my cell in humiliation.'

'Well, don't worry, you've got us with you now.' Blotto brandished his second-best cricket bat fervently. 'Twinks and I are a match for any number of the stenchers!'

'Really?' asked the laird, looking dubiously at the bat.

'Look, there's no time to fritter,' said Twinks. 'Let's put a jumping cracker under it and rescue Laetitia.'

'Good ticket,' Blotto agreed, turning towards the cell with the relevant key in his hand. Then he stopped. 'Think it'd be better if you freed her, Twinks me old cauliflower...'

'Why?'

Her brother blushed. 'Well, you know...Young women being rescued have a disturbing tendency to throw their arms round their liberators. And I'm deep enough into a gluepot with the Mater's plans to marry me off...'

Twinks understood immediately. She unlocked the door to greet a delighted Laetitia Melmont who immediately, ignoring her liberator, rushed out of the cell to throw her arms around Blotto.

'I knew our love was strong enough to defy any odds!' she boomed. 'Now nothing save death will ever part us again!'

Through Laetitia Melmont's all-encompassing embrace, Blotto caught his sister's eye. 'Sorry,' she mouthed.

Aloud, she asked Laetitia, 'Who imprisoned you here?'

'The only one I know by name was the pilot from Llanystwyth House.'

'Gerhardt Sachs?'

'Yes. The others were just men in uniform I had never met before,' she replied, her arms still wrapped around her reluctant paramour.

Once he had finally disentangled himself from the 'the Snitterings Ironing-Board' and introduced her to The McCluggan of McCluggan, Blotto said to the laird, 'You're the boddo with local knowledge. You'd better tell us the best way to get out of this place.'

'But surely,' Twinks intervened, 'our best route would be to go back the way we came? Out through the trapdoor. And down the steps to the beach. The League of the Crimson Hand don't know about that entrance.'

'Hoopee-doopee!' said Blotto. 'Give that pony a rosette!'

He would have said more, but was interrupted by heavy throat-clearing from The McCluggan of McCluggan. 'I'm afraid ye are wrong if ye imagine that the League o' the Crimson Hand are unaware of the sea entrance.'

'But none of the bad tomatoes stopped us when we came in that way,' protested Blotto.

'Did you nae think that was rather unco?' asked the laird.

' "Unco"?' echoed Blotto in bewilderment.

'Odd,' supplied his sister.

'Oh. Well, it was a bit—'

'You mean it was a trap?' Twinks asked the laird. As ever, her reasoning moved a lot faster than her brother's.

'Exactly that. The League hae been primed for your arrival since the moment you left Oban—or in fact some time before that. Once it was clear that Wellborough Choat had failed to sort oot their wee problem, they've been waiting for you here in Glenglower Castle. And I can guarantee there will now be a heavily armed presence at the mouth o' the cave on the beach.'

'That's a bit of a candle-snuffer,' said Blotto.

'So have you any ideas what we should do?' asked Twinks.

'Well now...' The McCluggan of McCluggan stroked his beard sagely. 'I do have a wee plan. It's a risk, but we're in a position where whatever we do is going to be a risk, so...' And he spelled out his plan for their escape.

Both Blotto and Twinks thoroughly approved of the notion, and the four of them moved as silently as they could into the interior of Glenglower Castle.

The McCluggan of McCluggan's plan appeared to work perfectly. As proposed, he took them a back way through the kitchens to a small chamber off the dining hall, where they discovered a bleary Gerhardt Sachs once again working his way down a bottle of brandy.

With speed surprising for a man of his age, The McCluggan of McCluggan quickly had one arm around the pilot's neck, while the other hand held the point of his *sgian dubh* against the man's throat. Gerhardt Sachs was too shocked for speech.

'Richt,' said the laird. 'We're ganging oot tae the court-yard, Sachs, with ye as our hostage. If any o' the League o' the Crimson Hand's guards raise a weapon tae us, my *sgian dubh* will slit your throat as easy as a pig's in an abattoir. I ken weel that the League willnae let ye die, because ye are the only body who kens the details o' their next major ootrage. So tae your feet and come wi's!'

Still silent, Gerhardt Sachs rose from his chair and let himself be led along the corridor to a large door which opened out on to the castle courtyard.

The space was full of League of the Crimson Hand guards. Close to, Blotto and Twinks could see the insignia of their orga-nization on the front of their dark grey uniforms. The moment the guards saw the emerging party they raised their rifles to their shoulders and took aim.

'Hauld your fire!' cried The McCluggan of McCluggan. 'One wee shot and mae hostage dees!'

The guards lowered their rifles, but still looked threat-ening. Tension was etched on the faces of four of the party which advanced across the courtyard. Only Blotto looked cheerful. In fact, he looked more than cheerful. He looked as though he had just been beatified by a particularly benevolent God. He saw nothing else in Glenglower Castle except, in the middle of the courtyard, his precious Lagonda. He couldn't prevent himself from murmuring an awestruck 'Toad-in-the-hole...'

It seemed as if it was the Lagonda towards which the laird was leading his hostage. In both Blotto and Twinks's minds the same image formed—of them inside the car with the two prisoners they had released, speeding southwards to the haven of Tawcester Towers.

But just before they reached the car, The McCluggan of McCluggan stopped still. He released his hold on Gerhardt Sachs, lowered his *sgian dubh* and looked around at the assembled guards with a smile.

'Well,' he said in a voice of the British upper classes, 'I think it's time for me to drop that dreadfully phony Scots accent.'

The guards roared with laughter, as they once again raised their rifles towards the intruders.

'Time too,' The McCluggan of McCluggan continued, 'to drop this little charade we've been playing.' He and Gerhardt Sachs moved away from the others as his acolytes laughed again. Then he bellowed out the order, 'Guards, put them in manacles and take them back down to the dungeons!'

'You mean,' asked a shell-shocked Twinks, 'that you...?'

The laird turned to face her and, favouring her with a thin smile, confirmed her worst fears by announcing, 'Yes. I, The McCluggan of McCluggan, am the Crimson Thumb!'

Chapter Twenty-eight

The Crimson Thumb

Following the instructions of their master, guards manacled the three intruders and led them back towards the interior of the castle. Just as they were about to enter, a call came out from The McCluggan of McCluggan—or, as they now should know him, the Crimson Thumb. 'Take the Melmont girl back to her cell! Leave the others with me. There is something I wish to show them.'

Blotto and Twinks may briefly have entertained hopes that they might be left alone with their adversary, giving them a greater chance of overpowering him in spite of their manacles, but such illusions were quickly dashed. A contingent of ten armed guards provided an escort as the pair were led in the wake of the Crimson Thumb into the castle by another door, and soon down a long spiral staircase. The deceitful laird led the way; five armed men between him and Blotto ruled out any possibility of attacking him. Five armed men behind Twinks equally effectively cut off the possibility of her escaping.

The spiral staircase went down deep into the solid crag on which Glenglower Castle had been built. Twinks was estimating that they must be at the same level as the cave through which they had entered the premises when suddenly the stairs ended. They passed through a thick metal door and found themselves on a smooth stone platform which looked out over another, larger cave.

This one too had a semicircular opening through which they could see pale moonlight shimmering on the waves outside. But this new cave was full of water, on whose surface floated large objects which could not be identified in the gloom.

'Let us allow our guests to see our pride and joy!' The Crimson Thumb's words were graciously phrased, but there was no doubt they represented a command.

And a command which was instantly obeyed. A guard must have flicked a switch, because the cave was suddenly flooded with light and revealed to be a natural aeroplane hangar. The large floating objects were revealed to be seaplanes, at least thirty of the beasts, all bristling with guns.

'Toad-in-the-hole!' said Blotto, impressed in spite of himself. 'Those are all Frimmelstopf Seefeuergewehrfliegflügels!'

'I congratulate you, Lyminster, on your skill in aircraft recognition. You have identified our air resources correctly. All of these belong to the League of the Crimson Hand, for us to use for whatever missions we see fit.'

At that moment Blotto and Twinks both noticed that on the fuselage of each seaplane was printed the large image of a Crimson Hand.

Blotto turned to face the evil genius of Glenglower Castle. 'What murdy devilment are you plotting, Thumb?'

His sister joined in. 'Yes, Thumb, what is the outrage that we heard Gerhardt Sachs and Wellborough Choat discussing at Llanystwyth House?'

Her question was answered by a mirthless laugh. 'I would not have replied to that question a few hours ago. But now my moment of triumph is so near, and your remaining time on earth is so short that, yes, I don't mind blowing my own trumpet a little. Guards!' he shouted. 'Chain the prisoners to the wall, retreat up the stairs, closing the door behind you—and do not return until I sound the siren!'

This time thoughts of staging an escape had hardly time to form in Blotto and Twinks's minds before they were dashed. The chains which were passed through their manacles and padlocked to the walls were heavy and strong.

When the three of them were alone, the Crimson Thumb chuckled again, with all the charm of a cobra taking a bead on a mesmerized mouse. 'I do not need to share my plans with everyone in the League. The pilots who will be flying these planes out in the morning know their duties. The rest of the riff-raff—those who are merely prepping the planes and guarding Glenglower Castle—are better kept in ignorance.'

'So what villainy are you planning?' demanded Twinks.

'Oh, very simple villainy, but very effective villainy. Presumably by now you know the aims of the League of the Crimson Hand?'

'To destroy the aristocracy of Europe and unsettle the governments of all its nations.'

'You are right, milady. How well you have done your research. So, given that that is the League's aim, where should they go to attack the aristocracy in this country?'

'Well,' replied Blotto, 'I suppose you go round all of the country houses, like you did at Snitterings and you...Well, I'll be snickered! You're not thinking of attacking Tawcester Towers, are you?'

But Twinks was, as usual, ahead of him. 'The House of Lords!' she said. 'You're thinking of attacking the House of Lords!'

'How quick you are, milady,' the Crimson Thumb acknowledged. 'You have a fine mind. A pity that an organ of such exquisite deductive powers will so soon be destroyed.'

'But just a minute—tomorrow! It's the Wednesday before Christmas! Tomorrow is the day when the highest number of members of the House of Lords will be present there! It's the day of the House of Lords Christmas lunch! Why, even our brother Loofah turns up for that!'

The Crimson Thumb nodded his head modestly. 'I too, you see, have done my research.'

'So,' demanded an astounded Blotto, 'you are planning to fly all these Seefeuergewehrfliegflügels down to London to turn their fire on the House of Lords?'

'Not just their fire. The planes down there have all been fitted with bomb bays.'

'You're going to bomb the spoffing House of Lords?'

'Exactly,' replied the Crimson Thumb with quiet satisfaction.

'But why?' asked Twinks. 'Why are you doing it? Someone in your position has nothing to gain from such an outrage. It's a betrayal of your own class. It goes against all the principles you have grown up with. The Marquis of Godalming told me that you loathed the very idea of Socialism.'

'And so I do. Socialism is not something I believe in.' There was a manic gleam in his eye as he grew more excited. 'The idea that everything should be shared equally—faugh, I almost retch to think of it. No, Socialism is simply the means by which I will achieve my ends. All of this riff-raff who surround me—this League of the Crimson Hand—oh, they all are obeying my orders because they believe that when the aristocrats are all dead, they will inherit the world. A just, equitable world in which everyone starts in life with the same privileges and potential.'

He laughed at the incongruity of the idea. 'Socialism will never be more than a sop that the rulers of the world throw to their disaffected commoners. But the League believes in me at this moment. They believe enough to carry out my plans to annihilate every member of this country's aristocracy. What they do not believe— or do not know—is that when they have served their purpose, when the new regime is in power, every man jack of them will be jailed for sedition and summarily executed.' The McCluggan of McCluggan let out an evil, self-congratulatory laugh.

Blotto was speechless. He tried to come up with words to express his outrage at what he was hearing, but was unable to do more than splutter.

His sister was more articulate. 'When you speak of the new regime, presumably you refer to a regime headed by yourself?'

He bowed his head in mock-compliment. 'Once again I admire your perspicacity. Yes, this country has a long tradition of being ruled by the nobility. Most of its people still have the mentality of serfs. They would no more know how to run a country than they would know which knife and fork to use at a formal dinner. They *like* kowtowing to the aristocracy. It's an instinct that is in their blood. So, when every other aristocrat in this country is dead, they will turn to the one who remains. And that one will be me—The McCluggan of McCluggan! First I will take over Great Britain—then the world!'

Twinks turned on him the full beam of her azure eyes. 'You're mad,' she said. 'Do you know that? You're stark staring mad.'

'And the murdiest kind of stencher,' added Blotto who had finally found his tongue.

The McCluggan of McCluggan did not reply. He turned to a row of buttons and pressed one. A siren sounded. As instructed, the guards returned. The McCluggan of McCluggan said nothing as they unchained his prisoners and manhandled them away up the spiral staircase.

He just looked with pride at the armoured fleet of seaplanes in the covered loch beneath him. And thought of the next day, the day that would bring the realization of all his ambitions.

Chapter Twenty-nine

Despair!

At least the three prisoners were put in the same cell. While this gave them the advantage of some company, it did also suggest the possibility that their planned incarceration would not be of long duration. And conjectures about what might end that incarceration were not ones that Twinks was about to share with Laetitia Melmont. No point in shattering the mood of ecstasy the girl derived from the idea that her beloved had risked life and limb to rescue her. And that the current interlude in a dungeon was merely the start of their new, inseparable life together.

The three of them were not actually chained to the wall, which was a minor blessing. But the manacles on their wrists and the locks on the door ruled out any possibility of escape.

'I'm really vinegared off,' Blotto kept saying. 'Absolutely fumacious. We're in the deepest gluepot yet created.'

'Don't worry,' Laetitia cooed volubly. 'Your heroism will see us through this challenge too, Blotto.'

He exchanged a wry look with his sister. Neither of them underestimated their current predicament. Even Twinks's normally unshakeable optimism was wobbling a little bit. But Blotto tossed a cheery 'Tickey-tockey' towards Laetitia to avert any potential hysterics.

He noticed the pensive expression on his sister's face. 'What's the bizz-buzz in that brainbox of yours, me old pineapple?'

'I was just trying to work out the timing.'

'Of what?'

'Of the Crimson Thumb's attack on the House of Lords.'

'He said "in the morning", so I assume he meant first thing.'

Twinks shook her head. 'No. He will not want the Seefeuergewehrfliegflügels to land anywhere between here and the Thames outside the House of Lords. He certainly won't want them to have to refuel. So they will fly straight from here to London. A trip which would take a standard Seefeuergewehrfliegflügel around two hours, though loaded with bombs they may fly a fraction slower. Well, the Lords never sit down to their Christmas lunch until at least one thirty.'

'How do you know that, Twinks me old umbrella stand?'

'I know that because Loofah has frequently told me how many whisky and sodas he has in the bar before going through to the dining room.'

'Tickey-tockey.'

'So, say two and a half hours…that means the seaplanes won't take off until about eleven. They may well come out of the cave into the open sea of the Firth before that, but I reckon their battle orders will be to take off at eleven.'

'I'm sorry, what are you talking about?' Laetitia Melmont's voice reverberated in the cramped space of the cell.

Blotto knew that holding back the information about the evil plans of the Crimson Thumb would be the chivalrous thing to do. But he also knew that, if Laetitia ever did find out about that particular act of chivalry, she would regard it simply as another demonstration of his undying love. So he told her.

She looked suitably shocked. 'What kind of a rotter would bomb the House of Lords while they're all having their Christmas lunch?'

'The kind of rotter we're up against. The Crimson Thumb, no less.'

'But good heavens!' Laetitia wailed loudly. 'My brother the Duke will be there tomorrow!'

The hysterics which Blotto had sought to avert were now unleashed at full volume. He looked at his sister and in both of their eyes was an unfamiliar look. It was one of despair.

'What's the time?' said Twinks.

He consulted the Accrington-Murphy Admiral Chronometer on his wrist. 'Just after midnight.'

Twinks's beautiful face screwed up with concentration. 'So we've got less than eleven hours to get ourselves out of this swamp-hole and thwart the villainies of the Crimson Thumb. Any thoughts how we're going to do it?'

Laetitia Melmont had by now managed to control her hysterics, and there was silence in the cell. It lasted for nearly an hour, the longest time that Blotto and Twinks had ever been awake in each other's company without speaking. Which was a measure of how close to despair they were.

And what finally spurred them to speech was sadly not one of them thinking of a way out of their predicament. It was the sound of footsteps approaching along the corridor.

'Rodents!' muttered Blotto. 'The stenchers are coming to get us. I'll try hiding behind the door, see if I can take some of them out. Oh, broken biscuits, I wish I had my cricket bat with me. Or even,' he continued with an affection he had never expected to feel for the object in question, 'my second-best cricket bat.'

The two girls were silent as he positioned himself. He wasn't going to be much use with his hands restrained, but at least the weight of his manacles might allow him to get in a few powerful blows at the Crimson Thumb's guards.

The footsteps outside stopped, and they heard the ring of keys being lifted from its hook on the wall. Then the key was inserted into the lock of their cell. An eternity seemed to pass before they heard the key turn in the lock, saw the door slowly open as a man stepped in.

Blotto leapt forward with manacled hands upraised.

'Great dithering dragonflies!' said a familiar voice.

It was Jerome Handsomely.

'How on earth did you get here?' asked Twinks.

'I saw that kite you'd left flying for me. Used it as a marker. Very crumpety that you'd left it by that flat field. Perfect tarmac-tickling area for me to land my crate. Well done, whoever thought of that little wrinkle.'

Blotto looked across at his sister and saw a sight which he had very rarely witnessed before. Twinks actually looked embarrassed. She may have kept her views mostly to herself, but he knew she'd thought his idea of the kite was complete guff. And now he was in the unusual position of being superior to her.

In his moment of glory Blotto could not restrain himself. Reverting to the language of their nursery, he thumbed his nose and said, 'So snubbins to you, Twinks!'

Chapter Thirty

The Battle in the Air

Jerome Handsomely, it transpired, had checked through Glenglower Castle before coming to their rescue. 'Absolutely snuffled-up to tell you that all the slimers are busy prepping the seaplanes. None of the bally stopcock-twiddlers are guarding anything.'

'Not even the Lagonda?' asked Blotto breathlessly.

'Standing in the middle of the courtyard without a single one of the tinkety-tonkers in sight.'

'Hoopee-doopee! So long as my cricket bat's still there it'll all be creamy éclair!'

'Come on, we must put a jumping cracker under it!' urged Twinks. 'The guards won't be prepping the seaplanes for ever.'

'Good ticket, Twinks. Let's shift our shimmies and get off the prems before anyone gets a whiff that the Stilton's iffy! Have you got a plan, Jerome?'

'Yes, me old propeller-winder—and a booming good one! We'll twang off the tarmac soonest and I'll fly down to a private aerodrome two o'clock north of London. And when the Crimson Thumb's seaplanes approach, I'll be ready for the tinkety-tonkers. We'll have the crumpetiest dogfight since records began!'

'There are over thirty of them,' cautioned Twinks.

Jerome Handsomely twirled his moustache. 'Kind of odds I like! And if I end up as Pilot Flambé…well, at least I'll have had the satisfaction of laying down my life for you, Twinks.'

It wasn't the moment for her to argue this point again, so all she said was, 'How many can you take in your crate, Jerome?'

'Three top weight, as you know from our little flip to Wales.'

'Four?'

He shook his head. 'You know how cramped we were that time.'

'Yes.'

'Don't worry,' said Blotto. 'I'll drive the Lagonda!'

'Oh, wonderful!' simpered Laetitia Melmont. 'You'll drive me back to Snitterings—and from this moment on we'll continue to be together for ever!'

Blotto realized he had yet again somehow given further proof of his non-existent love for the girl, but now wasn't the moment to start the difficult process of disillusioning her. 'Come on, we'll all get in the Lag,' he cried, 'and I'll take you and Twinks to your plane, Jerome!'

When they reached it, the courtyard remained as silent as the pilot had described it. He and Blotto moved quietly towards the Lagonda. Cautiously they pushed the magnificent car out through the main gate of the castle and some way down its approach road before they both leapt in and Blotto fired the engine.

'If I drive through the night,' he said, 'I should get to the House of Lords just about the time the peers are all quaffing their pre-prandials. I'll warn the poor old thimbles that the Seefeuergewehrfliegflügels are on their way!'

'Hopefully,' said Jerome Handsomely, 'I should have taken most of the stopcock-twiddlers out by then.'

They had just arrived by his Accrington-Murphy Painted Lady Biplane. It stood at the end of a flat field.

'Booming crumpety of you to find this natural landing strip—and leave the kite to mark it,' said the pilot.

Blotto caught his sister's eye and vouchsafed her a smile of superiority.

Jerome Handsomely pointed out the pair of Accrington-Murphy machine guns he'd had mounted on his plane's fuselage either side of the cockpit. 'Those two little jujubes'll prove more than a match for that shoddy Continental Frimmelstopf technology,' he asserted.

'Toad-in-the-hole...' said Blotto suddenly. His triumph over Twinks in the matter of using the kite as a direction-finder had boosted his confidence sufficiently for him to have had another of his rare ideas. 'Jerome, I've just had a spoffingly brilliant notion that'll really come up with the silverware.'

'What is it, me old propeller-twiddler?'

'It's what they call a presumptive strike.'

The pilot looked confused until Twinks explained, 'I think Blotto means a pre-emptive strike.'

'Oh, trucky-trockle. Well, me old poached egg, tell me what your notion is zappity-ping.'

'My notion is,' said Blotto, slowly and with considerable pride, 'that you fly in to where the Seefeuergewehrfliegflügels are being prepped and you machine-gun the lot of them before they're even in the air.'

'Yes, I can see that would tick the clock...but there is one small wasp in the jam.'

'What?' asked Blotto, affronted that his brilliant scheme was not being accepted straight away.

'The Seefeuergewehrfliegflügels,' Jerome Handsomely explained gently, 'are *sea*planes. My Accrington-Murphy Painted Lady is a biplane. There's no way I could manoeuvre my crate in through that narrow entrance, destroy the fleet and get her out again. I'd end up in the briny. It'd be a case of not so much Pilot Flambé as Pilot à la Marinade.'

Blotto was reluctant for his brilliant idea to be so summarily thrown aside. 'But if by ending up in the briny you were effectively laying down your life for my sister, then surely—'

'No,' Twinks interrupted firmly. 'If Jerome insists on laying down his life for me, then I don't want it to happen until we know that we have thwarted the Crimson Thumb's plans to bomb the House of Lords.'

'Oh, broken biscuits,' said Blotto disconsolately.

So they stuck to their original plan. Blotto and the adoring Laetitia set out for London in the Lagonda, while Jerome and Twinks flew south in the Accrington-Murphy Painted Lady Biplane to the secret airstrip that he knew.

It might have been thought that the series of dogfights in which Jerome Handsomely shot down most of the Seefeuergewehrfliegflügels of the Crimson Thumb would have been proudly recorded in the annals of our island history, but in fact no records of the encounters exist. This was due to the sensitivity of the then government, which had no wish to expose its own frailties to the general public.

The fact that the League of the Crimson Hand should have got so close to destroying the entire aristocracy of the British Isles was not one which Downing Street wished to advertise. It reflected badly on the security they had in place at the time.

Nor did they wish the general public to be aware that the threat had been averted, not by their own air defences, but by the efforts of one amateur in a private plane, assisted only by a beautiful young woman with a title. It has been the ambition of governments through the ages to maintain—frequently in the teeth of the evidence—that they are in control.

Suffice it to say then that, when the Crimson Thumb's thirty Seefeuergewehrfliegflügels approached London in a 'V' formation, they found Jerome Handsomely's Accrington-

Murphy Painted Lady Biplane ready for them. His tactics were carefully planned. The Crimson Thumb, sitting gleefully in the cockpit of the leading plane, did not anticipate any opposition to his attack, and was therefore surprised to see Handsomely's kite coming straight towards his seaplane. By the time the League's gunners were in position, the two planes were on collision course, and the distance between them was diminishing at electric speed.

At that moment Jerome Handsomely's Accrington-Murphy machine gun began to spit out deadly lead to the left and Twinks's Accrington-Murphy machine gun did the same to the right. Their actions showed up the impracticality of having planes flying in a 'V' formation. Given the exceptional firepower of the British-designed and made Accrington-Murphy, bullets ripped into the Seefeuergewehrfliegflügels on either side of the Crimson Thumb's, and as each one dropped down, it revealed the target of the next plane in line. And so on, until twenty-six of the enemy fleet were spiralling down in flames to embed themselves in the open countryside of Hertfordshire.

By then of course a head-on crash between the biplane and the Crimson Thumb's kite seemed inevitable. But with a cry of 'Quick tickle of the button-box!', Jerome Handsomely flicked a control and his kite lifted above the leading Seefeuergewehrfliegflügel, taking a bit of the enemy's propeller with it as a souvenir.

'This is booming good fun!' crowed the pilot. 'Now let's take out the stragglers!'

This was a tougher task, because the biplane was flying away from its targets and had to turn round to catch them. And all the time they were getting closer to their destination of the House of Lords, where they would unload their cargo of death.

But Jerome Handsomely and Twinks did a tidy mopping-up operation and by the time the Houses of Parliament hove into view, only two of the Seefeuergewehrfliegflügels remained in the air. The crippled one which contained the Crimson

Thumb was still aloft, but had been slowed down, so that the other flew ahead of it, getting ever closer to fulfilling the criminal mastermind's evil plans.

This leading plane now became Jerome Handsomely's primary target. Time enough to deal with the Crimson Thumb when the more immediate danger had been dealt with. He could see the approaching Thames with the tower of Big Ben rising up beside it. The thought of all that Perpendicular Gothic splendour being destroyed was more than his true-blue British heart could stomach (if a heart is actually capable of stomaching anything).

'The chicken-livered ballcock-twiddler's getting a bit too close for my liking! I'm going to knock the slimer off his bearings!' Handsomely roared at Twinks as he set his biplane on another collision course.

The pilot of the Seefeuergewehrfliegflügel saw the danger and slightly changed direction, so that he was no longer going straight towards the Houses of Parliament. But disaster was only deferred for a moment. The enemy kite swung round in a wide circle to position itself on a course which in seconds would be directly over its target.

Jerome Handsomely took his biplane in a mirror image of the same manoeuvre, so that the two aircraft were once again approaching each other at furious speed. The spot where they would meet was directly above the House of Lords.

'Twinks, give them everything we've got with the Accrington-Murphys!' bellowed her admirer.

The pilot of the Seefeuergewehrfliegflügel must have had the same idea, because deadly fire blazed from its barrels as the two planes roared towards each other. Twinks heard the sound of the cockpit glass shattering around her.

'Nothing else for it, me old iced bun!' roared Jerome Handsomely. 'I'm going to have to bounce the tinkety-tonker!'

As he had done with the Crimson Thumb's plane, he waited until collision seemed inevitable, then made the deftest of flicks to the controls. 'Hang on to your hairdo, Twinks!' he shouted.

Whereas he'd avoided the previous clash by flying over the approaching plane, this time he diverted to one side. There was a sickening impact as the biplane's wings smashed against the single wing of the Seefeuergewehrfliegflügel. Handsomely's kite shuddered as he fought to regain control, screeching low over the roofs of Westminster.

But, bad though the effect had been on them, Twinks, looking back, could see how much worse their enemy had suffered. Knocked off course and crippled by the crash, the Seefeuergewehrfliegflügel was spinning down towards the Thames. It must have dropped its bombs because loud bangs were heard and columns of water shot up in the air above the ridge of the Houses of Parliament's roofs.

Then their opponent's spiralling plane disappeared in flames over the same roofs. There was a moment of silence, followed by a huge detonation, and a high column of steam rose up to the air.

'Now to get the Crimson Thumb!' Jerome Handsomely gasped, as if in pain.

'Are you all right?' asked Twinks anxiously.

'Trucky-trockle!' he assured her.

Somehow managing to get his damaged biplane back on course, he flew back to the House of Lords, expecting to face a new attack from the remaining Seefeuergewehrfliegflügel. But there was no sign of the Crimson Thumb's plane.

Then they heard an engine roar from behind them. With difficulty Jerome Handsomely looked round. 'Oh, wingless biplanes!' he screeched at Twinks. 'The slimers are making for Buckingham Palace!'

Chapter Thirty-one

Regicide?

Blotto's Lagonda had driven like the wind from Glenglower Castle, stopping only for necessary refuelling. He had hardly spoken at all, not wishing to say anything that his passenger might interpret as further proof of his undying adoration for her. But Laetitia Melmont had sat quite happily beside him, knowing from extensive reading of romantic fiction that some loves were too great for words.

Leaving behind a trail of other cars, farm carts and cyclists forced into ditches, they made good time till they reached the outskirts of London. Here the inevitable buildup of traffic slowed them down, but only a bit. Blotto didn't change the style of driving which he adopted when speeding through the narrow lanes of Tawcestershire. His attitude was that there probably wouldn't be anything coming in the opposite direction and, if there was, the approaching vehicle should recognize his superior status and get out of the way. This caused a good few other vehicles to smash into each other, but the Lagonda retained its pristine, undented beauty.

The trouble was that, though Blotto knew the Tawcestershire lanes like the back of his hand, he was an infrequent visitor to London and his sense of geography in the capital was a little vague. Possessed of the instinctive male reluctance to ask for directions, he tended to find his way by driving round aimlessly in the confidence that he would eventually reach his destination.

It was due to this hit-and-miss approach that one thirty— the hour when the Crimson Thumb's attack on the House of Lords was expected—found him frustratedly parked with a road map unfolded all over his steering wheel.

'Are you telling me you don't know where the Houses of Parliament are?' asked Laetitia Melmont, unable to believe that the man she was about to marry could be capable of such ignorance.

'Well, I sort of vaguely know,' said Blotto, warming to the coldness in her tone. If Laetitia was disappointed to find him deficient in geographical skills, she might be less keen on marrying him. Then if he demonstrated a few other skills that he was deficient in, which wouldn't be too difficult...

But the smile that she bestowed on him strangled that hope in the cradle. Though he didn't know it, Laetitia Melmont was encouraged to find flaws in her future mate. That meant he could become a *project* for her, that she could *mould* him. Blotto was not aware how much women relish such challenges.

But the situation was serious. They'd made good time all the way from Glenglower Castle and now they were within a few minutes of their rescue mission's destination and Blotto didn't know how to get there. He turned back to the confusing jumble of streets on his map.

But his attention was snatched away by the sound of an approaching aircraft. He looked up through the Lagonda's windshield to see a Seefeuergewehrfliegflügel flying low towards him. He turned to see a familiar building and for the first time realized that he had chosen to park outside Buckingham Palace.

The plane was very close. It seemed to be using the Mall as a guide to lead it straight to the palace. By the time Blotto was out of the Lagonda the kite was directly overhead, then just shaving the top of the recent Queen Victoria Memorial, and doing the same to the palace roof before shooting off into the distance. Just a sighting trip. The plane would return.

Blotto rushed to the palace gates, having thoughtfully taken both his second-best cricket bat and his precious original one with him. The red-coated guardsmen with bearskins stood unmoving in their sentry boxes; they were trained not to react to anything. But inside the gates there was a confusion of policemen and soldiers running around in panic.

Why the Seefeuergewehrfliegflügel had not released its load of bombs on its first foray no one knew (well, no one actually knew till later that it had a load of bombs). Perhaps its minor collision with Jerome Handsomely's biplane had caused some jamming of the bomb bays. The only thing certain was that the plane was already circling for another attack on Buckingham Palace. It was wheeling around, again seeking out the Mall as a directional aid.

With no thought of danger—or, as usual, of much else— Blotto began to climb the main gates of the palace. This time the Seefeuergewehrfliegflügel was flying even lower. Its intention was no longer to bomb its target, but to crash into it. Blotto looked back to see that the Royal Standard was flying. The King was inside the building. The Crimson Thumb's plan was now neither more nor less than regicide.

Blotto reached the high point of the gates. Clasping his legs round the central uprights to give him a firm footing, he waited with one cricket bat in each hand, his beloved one in the right and the second-best in his left. The approaching plane's guns were blazing. He felt bullets shave through his thatch of blond hair and take chunks of tweed from his suit.

But he held his ground with the pride that the Lyminsters had shown on innumerable battlefields. The Seefeuergewehrfliegflügel was getting lower and lower; in a second the propeller would have his head off.

But Blotto stiffened his sinews and stayed put, feeling the same excitement as he did before that final six which had given him his unbeaten hundred and seventy-six when he clinched the Eton and Harrow match.

Just at the moment when death seemed inevitable he threw up his second-best cricket bat to tangle into the plane's propeller. Instantly he seemed to have both hands on the other bat and with that he made a glorious upward shot which clanged against the plane's fuselage.

It was not much, but it was enough to change the plane's trajectory. The nose flicked upwards and the kite again missed the palace roofs by inches. A few seconds later from Green Park came the loud report of the Seefeuergewehrfliegflügel smashing into smithereens. A plume of dark smoke rose behind Buckingham Palace.

'Well,' said Blotto, as he got into the Lagonda, 'time we went and checked on the bizz-buzz at the House of Lords.'

Laetitia Melmont's eyes were swimming with admiration. 'My hero!' she murmured.

Oh, broken biscuits, thought Blotto. How am I going to get this chock out of the cogwheel?

Chapter Thirty-two

Twinks Takes Control

In the crippled Accrington-Murphy Painted Lady Biplane Twinks and Jerome Handsomely heard the explosion from Green Park and he flew over to see what had happened. Though they did not know then of Blotto's part in the plane's destruction, they were both satisfied that the threat from the Crimson Thumb had been finally thwarted.

Another thing they did not know at the time was that when the wreckage of the Seefeuergewehrfliegflügel was examined (before being quickly removed by government agencies) only one body was found, that of the pilot. Somehow The McCluggan of McCluggan has escaped. It seemed unlikely that he could have survived the inferno of the crash, so he was reckoned to have bailed out with a parachute before the attacks on Buckingham Palace, and somehow disappeared into the busy streets of London.

Which meant of course that the defeat of his fleet of seaplanes did not spell the end of the Crimson Thumb, and that he might reappear at some later date with another dastardly plan to take over the world.

But such thoughts did not concern Twinks. She was more worried about Jerome Handsomely, who had taken a couple of bullets in the chest when the glass of his cockpit had been shattered by enemy fire. He was bleeding profusely and soon became too weak to control the damaged biplane.

'You take over the button-box, me old iced bun. I'll talk you down.'

With difficulty they changed places and Twinks took the controls. 'Are you sure you're all right, Jerome?' she asked.

'Oh yes, just a flesh wound,' he assured her, coughing blood the while.

'Where are we flying to?'

'Croydon Aerodrome. Plenty of away-chockers there who'll get this crate back to battle fitness quicker than a doctor's bill. Touch of left on the helmrod.'

Twinks duly gave a touch of left on the helmrod and the plane readjusted its trajectory. She had never flown a plane before, but she found Jerome Handsomely's instructions easy to follow. The only thing that worried her was that, the further they went, the fainter and fainter his voice became.

Still doing exactly as he told her, she made a perfect landing at Croydon Aerodrome. 'Booming good show,' he murmured. 'Lot of professional away-chockers I know wouldn't have tickled the tarmac as gently as that.'

Expertly, Twinks taxied the biplane alongside a hangar and then looked at Jerome Handsomely. He was very pale. The blood had soaked his khaki shirt and was now pouring down his leather jacket. 'We need to get you to a doctor as quick as a lizard's lick.'

'Not worth the tribulation,' he sighed. 'I'm a busted flush. Crocking business, life, ain't it?'

'But, Jerome, I'm sure you can be saved,' said Twinks, more for form's sake than anything else. She didn't really think that a likely outcome.

'Don't fret. All trucky-trockle with me. You see, I've got what I wanted,' he gasped.

'What, Jerome?'

'I'm laying down my life for you, Twinks.'

'Well, that's very sweet of you—and much appreciated.' The pilot's eyes were beginning to glaze over. 'I love you, Twinks,' he murmured.

Now many women, whatever the precise nature of their feelings towards him, would have eased Jerome Handsomely's passage into eternity by saying 'I love you too.' But Twinks was very particular about emotional issues like that. She didn't love him, so she didn't say anything, just cradled his body as she felt the last spasm of life shudder through it and heard the sound of his death rattle.

And she really thought her amour with Jerome Handsomely had been one of the more successful ones of her life.

Chapter Thirty-three

Justice Done

Brother and sister were reunited at Tawcester Towers. As was her wont, once she had thrown away the inevitable accumulation of love letters which had built up during her absence, Twinks wrote up a full dossier of the investigation. This was quickly passed over to Inspector Trumbull and Sergeant Knatchbull. As was their wont, after only one reading of the document, Inspector Trumbull and Sergeant Knatchbull had convinced themselves that they had solved the case themselves.

The innocence of Corky Froggett in the matter of the Dowager Duchess of Melmont's death having been firmly established, he was released. Master and chauffeur were happily reunited, though Blotto did curb Corky's excessive protestations about how willing he would have been to lay his life on the line for him. Blotto felt he'd heard enough of that sort of stuff to last a lifetime from Jerome Handsomely.

He didn't feel the ease which normally enveloped him as soon as he entered his ancestral home. Laetitia Melmont had come with him to Tawcester Towers and he knew it was only a matter of time before the Dowager Duchess issued him with his matrimonial marching orders.

In retrospect, the adventure which had just concluded couldn't have been worse from Blotto's point of view. Not only had he succeeded in rescuing Laetitia Melmont, he had also spent the best part of a day driving with her from Glenglower Castle to London. Ruefully he remembered the Mater telling him that 'Catholics are even less tolerant than normal people of unchaperoned young persons of different genders being alone together.' Oh, broken biscuits, there was no way he was going to escape marriage this time.

The summons didn't come as soon as he expected. The Dowager Duchess had invited Laetitia Melmont to stay at Tawcester Towers as long as she wished, which was in itself a bad sign. And during her visit, Laetitia was encouraged to spend as much time as possible alone with Blotto. He grew gloomier and gloomier at the inevitability of a lifetime's shackling to 'the Snitterings Ironing-Board'. He looked at the example of Loofah and Sloggo, and groaned.

Finally one day he heard from Twinks that the Dowager Duchess had summoned Laetitia Melmont to meet her in the Blue Morning Room. This was ominous. There was a daunting formality about the Blue Morning Room; it was from there that most of the Dowager Duchess's pronouncements were issued. And the Dowager Duchess was something of a specialist in pronouncements.

The two women seemed to be incarcerated in there for a surprisingly long time. Sorting through financial details, Blotto thought wretchedly. But eventually Grimshaw summoned him from the billiard room to join the ladies.

The Dowager Duchess immediately announced that she was going to bully the cook about dinner. She left the Blue Morning Room with the ominous instruction that: 'I'm sure you young people have a lot to talk about.'

'Yes, I'm sure we do,' agreed Blotto miserably after his mother had left. Even in the dungeon of Glenglower Castle he hadn't felt such restriction of his freedom as he did at that minute.

'Blotto,' said Laetitia Melmont, 'your mother is expecting you to ask me to marry you.'

'I know,' he concurred pitifully. 'Do you actually want me to go through the business of going down on one knee and asking you and all that rombooley, or are we just going to accept the Mater's word on it?'

'You can ask me if you like,' replied Laetitia.

Blotto got down on one knee and tried to think of the right way to do it. Last thing he wanted to do was to offend the old fruitbat, but somehow the words clogged his throat like lumpy porridge.

'Erm...' he said eventually. It always seemed to be a safe opening conversational gambit.

'Before you say anything, Blotto, there's something I need to say.'

Oh, broken biscuits, he thought, here we go. No doubt a set of rules that I'll have to obey once the noose is actually round my neck. Cut down on the brandy and soda, less billiards, fewer days hunting...He knew of other poor old thimbles who'd had their pleasures curtailed by matrimony in similar ways. Some of them would have had more freedom of movement in a plaster cast.

'The thing is,' Laetitia boomed, 'I have had a lot of opportunity in the last weeks to think about love.'

'Oh, have you?' Blotto tried unsuccessfully to keep the gloom out of his voice.

'And I have decided that, of all human beings, Blotto, you are the only one that I have ever loved.'

Rodents, he thought, this is it. A sentence involving the words 'slaughter' and 'lamb' came unbidden into his head.

'But, Blotto, in this world human love is not the only kind of love.'

What the strawberries was she on about?

'You know, Blotto, that I am a Catholic.'

'Tickey-tockey. Yes, and the Mater said that Catholics have some very odd ideas when it comes to...' He hesitated, not wishing to quote his mother exactly. '...er, marriage and all that kind of rombooley,' he finished feebly.

'The fact is, Blotto, that my faith is very strong...'

'Good ticket.'

'Is your faith strong, Blotto?'

He made do with another 'Erm...' Like most of the aristocracy, Blotto was robustly Church of England, a comfortable situation which did not involve believing in anything in particular. He filled the ensuing silence with that reliable conversational fall-back, a 'Well...'

'The fact is,' Laetitia Melmont suddenly blurted out, 'I want to become a nun!'

'Oh?' said Blotto, hardly daring to believe that his ears had served him right.

'It is something I have considered for a long time, but while I was incarcerated by the League of the Crimson Hand I had the opportunity to read deeply in the Catholic divines.'

'Did you, by Jove?'

'Ignatius Loyola, Thomas Aquinas...'

'Oh, the horse boddo, yes.'

'...and I have decided that I have a vocation, to renounce worldly pleasures and devote my life to the contemplation of the Almighty.'

'Ah, right, well, yes. I gather it does take some people that way.'

'I know how much pain my decision will cause you, Blotto.'

'Oh, well, I'll probably pull through," he replied, hope reopening within his heart like a flower. Then, realizing that that might sound too readily accepting, he added soberly, 'Though it'll take a spoffing long time.'

'Perhaps after your disappointment,' Laetitia bellowed, 'you too will find a vocation.'

'Well, I've got one, actually. Hunting.'

'I meant a religious vocation.'

'Did you? Well, yes, I suppose I might develop one. Never say you're out of luck till the croupier's got your last chip, eh?'

While he was with Laetitia, Blotto managed to keep his expression that of a man all of whose romantic hopes have just been dashed. But the minute he got out of the Blue Morning Room, he was unable to contain a gazelle-like leap across the hall and an ecstatic 'Hooppee-doopee!'

He thought of going to share the good news with Twinks, but this was something on a scale that transcended the mere love of siblings. For a moment he considered going to stroke and sniff and commune with the linseed smell of his cricket bat. But then he decided the most satisfying course would be to go and share his exaltation with his hunter Mephistopheles.

And so life at Tawcester Towers returned to its torpid normality. Loofah, unaware of how close he and his peers had come to obliteration, got on with the thankless task of trying to impregnate Sloggo with a boy. Twinks, rather bored by the latest round of men swearing undying devotion to her, wrote to Professor Erasmus Holofernes to send her a novel in Serbo-Croat that she wanted to translate into Mandarin.

And Blotto? Oh, he went hunting.